THE NOVELIZATION

DISNEY

DESCENDANTS 3

THE NOVELIZATION

Adapted by Carin Davis

Based on *Descendants 3*, written by

Josann McGibbon & Sara Parriott

DISNEY PRESS

Los Angeles • New York

Printed in the United States of America
First Hardcover Edition, July 2019
First Paperback Edition, July 2019
1 3 5 7 9 10 8 6 4 2
FAC-025438-19165

Library of Congress Control Number: 2019933992

ISBN 978-1-368-05352-5

For more Disney Press fun, visit www.disneybooks.com
Visit DisneyChannel.com

SUSTAINABLE
FORESTRY
INITIATIVE
Certified Chain of Custody
Promoting Sustainable Forestry
www.sfiprogram.org
SFI-01054
The SFI label applies to the text stock

To King Ben, for taking a chance on four villain kids

from the Isle and changing our lives forever

CHAPTER ONE

Hi, Mal here. Remember me? Daughter of Maleficent. Wicked wild child of the Isle turned proper lady of the court. Right? I know.

At first, I tried way too hard to impress Ben and all of Auradon and totally lost myself. I was suffocating under all those layers of pale pink tulle. It wasn't me. So I broke up with Ben, fled home to the Isle, and rediscovered my roots (literally—Dizzy gave my lame blond hair a fierce purple makeover). My lifelong nemesis, Uma (who I call "Shrimpy"), the daughter of Ursula, and her scallywag gang of wannabe pirates weren't too happy with my return—old turf wars and whatnot. Then there was the pirate duel, which was kinda legendary.

AS WAS THE ROYAL COTILLION. UMA TRANSFORMED INTO
A GIANT OCTOPUS AND THREATENED MY FRIENDS. I WENT ALL
FIRE-BREATHING DRAGON ON HER AND SAVED AURADON. UMA IS
SCARED OFF FOR NOW, BUT ALL HER ANTICS MADE ME REALIZE
THAT I DO BELONG AS LADY OF AURADON. I CAN'T DENY
THAT I'LL ALWAYS BE PART ISLE, THOUGH. THE TRUE ME LIES
SOMEWHERE IN THE SPACE BETWEEN. THE OTHER AMAZING
THING THAT HAPPENED AT COTILLION? EVIE ASKED BEN TO
HELP BRING OVER MORE VKS FROM THE ISLE TO AURADON, TO
GIVE THEM THE SAME CHANCE HE GAVE US. AND, WELL . . .

CHAPTER TWO

MOTHER ALWAYS SAID IT WAS GOOD TO BE BAD. I CAN'T BELIEVE SHE WAS ACTUALLY RIGHT ABOUT SOMETHING....

At dawn, a ragtag paperboy rode his rusted-out bicycle down a squalid Isle street. He careened over a teetering makeshift ramp and past a run-down tenement with *Long Live Evil* graffitied across its wall. The young street rat pulled a copy of the *Troubled Times* newspaper out of his grungy messenger bag and tossed it over his shoulder. "Hey, check it out," he yelled to the other kids in the square.

A curly-haired imp in a rumpled pink dress scampered to pick up the paper. "Oh my gosh, oh my gosh! Look at this!" the girl exclaimed in shock. The big bold headline splashed across the front page read VK DAY IS HERE! 4 MORE TO GO ASHORE.

"It's VK Day," she squealed to the crowd of kids who'd gathered around for a peek at the paper. "I want them to pick me so bad."

A detailed article described the progressive new holiday established by His Royal Highness King Ben and villain kid turned successful fashion designer Evie. For the first time, any villain kid could apply to attend the kingdom's esteemed Auradon Prep. The new class would be handpicked in person from among the Isle applicants by the original villain kids: Mal, Evie, Carlos, and Jay. Then, one week later, King Ben and the VKs would be back to escort the lucky students to Auradon to start the new school year.

Many of the Isle kids had never lifted a pencil or sat behind a desk, let alone brought their teacher an unpoisoned apple. The hope was that the chosen students, like the inaugural class of VKs, would thrive amid the opportunities Auradon had to offer.

As the paperboy tossed another paper nowhere close to anyone's door, Mal, Evie, Carlos, and Jay rounded the dilapidated street corner in step. Since making their own way in Auradon, the four friends had become folk heroes to the villain kids still stuck on the Isle. And now they were back in their old hood with good news—make that *great* news.

They ducked under clotheslines heavy with drip-drying rags and yelled for the Isle kids to rise and shine—well, as much shining as could happen in the sunless place. It was time for all the young VKs to get up and step up; Auradon Prep was waiting.

Mal and her close-knit squad strode with confidence down the grimy street and into a cobblestoned square now named Mal Court. A group of inspired villain offspring had renamed the shabby square after seeing a clip of Mal on TV. The broadcast showed Lady Mal at Cotillion giving a public shout-out to her Isle roots. The Isle kids knew she hadn't forgotten them.

Mal turned toward her three best friends, bursting with excitement, as her purple hair, tinted a more violet hue than ever before, flew behind her in the wind. That day was going to be epic. She slayed in leather leggings, wedge high-top sneakers, and a fitted tailcoat. On the back of her coat were sculptured leather dragon wings that caged her signature two-dragon icon.

Evie, daughter of Evil Queen, flashed a dazzling smile at Mal. After months of diligent planning and painstaking prep, VK Day was finally here. Evie exuded confidence and authority as her blue suede boots hit the pavement. She swept down the street like the leader she was, the essence of style in her short blue leather skirt and matching jacket with her heart-and-crown emblem painted on the back.

With his long dark brown hair and mischievous smile, Jay, the son of Jafar, wove easily through his old stomping ground. He radiated attitude, with his sleeveless leather vest and leather pants showing off his athletic build. Jay glanced at Carlos and laughed. They were about to change some lives forever. What an amazing feeling.

Carlos, son of Cruella De Vil, rolled through the street, energized by the big day to come. Once thought of as puppy dog cute, with his face full of freckles, Carlos had grown up and was now coming into his own. He was also super edgy. All the VKs were. He had shocking white hair with black roots and wore a red, white, and black jacket with a flipped-up fur collar. He'd come a long way from the boy who was afraid of everything—particularly his mother and puppies—and he couldn't wait to pass his good fortune forward.

At the end of the crumbling street, Mal, Evie, Carlos, and Jay broke apart and fanned out in every direction, eager to get the word out about VK Day. They headed down dusty alleys littered with over-turned wheelbarrows and snaked through dismal passageways filled with desolate shacks. Jay literally shouted the news from the tin rooftops. They urged all the villain kids they could find to hit the streets. VK Day offered a chance for any Isle urchin who wanted to be like them. And didn't everyone want to be like them?

Mal moved through a courtyard, doing her best to spread the word. She wanted these kids to know they had the opportunity to join her in Auradon and live their best life. A young girl in a threadbare pur-ple dress pushed open her window and waved her Auradon application excitedly at Mal. Mal looked up and saw kids in every broken window and rotting doorframe around the courtyard gripping their applications. She smiled, realizing just how many next-gen VKs were choosing to be good.

While Mal circled through the courtyard, Carlos stormed through the Isle orphanage, with its rickety bunks and walls with chipped paint. He bounded by a plaque that read CARLOS HOUSE, and he chuckled. He still couldn't believe these little mischief-makers looked up to him, but it warmed his heart. He yanked a ratty blanket off a sleeping boy, who jolted awake. The boy stared in awe for several seconds when he saw Carlos standing at the foot of his bed, then grabbed his application from beneath his lumpy pillow and pushed it into Carlos's gloved hand.

Down the block, Evie stood beneath the weathered CURL UP AND DYE sign and waited with giddy anticipation. She raised her gaze to the sign, which depicted a giant pair of scissors crisscrossing a faded perfume bottle, just to check that it was real. She'd imagined that moment again and again, ever since she'd dispatched royal couriers to that very spot with a scroll the past spring. But this time it wasn't a daydream. Dizzy Tremaine, still holding her broom, bolted out of the shabby salon's double doors wearing a patchwork dress and nightcap. She hugged Evie, whom she looked up to like a big sister, and the two girls marveled at what that day meant for kids on the Isle.

Evie and Dizzy talked over each other, trying to catch up on months of conversation in mere minutes, as they strutted down a back street to meet up with Mal, Jay, and Carlos. Evie was thrilled to see so many aspiring students. She hoped there were even a few fellow chemistry fans in the crowd. VK Day had truly turned out to be everything she'd envisioned and so much more.

The rowdy group walked by Jay, who was pumped about giving back to other misguided Isle kids. To kids like these, Jay was a hero. He was a celebrated athlete and team leader. Jay accepted applications from several kids and went off in search of Mal.

Mal had returned to the courtyard and was spray-painting *VK Day!* in bright purple and green hues across a battered old garage door while Evie looked on. She stepped back and admired her art. Who said graffiti couldn't beautify the neighborhood? She slid open the just-tagged panel and a wave of bedraggled VKs, all clutching applications, rushed out wildly. Mal scanned the group of wharf rats and noticed a few key kids were missing. Not on her watch. Mal's aim was for every offspring of evil to get a shot at life in Auradon. She hurried back onto the street toward the Isle's bustling bayou.

With its strings of brightly colored lights and notes of jazz music in the air, the vibrant French Quarter district was one of Mal's favorite Isle locales. In the heart of the jumping neighborhood, Dr. Facilier's feisty daughter, Celia, set up shop under a FORTUNES TOLD sign covered in colorful question marks. The tween had shoulder-length bouncy red curls and wore ripped jeans adorned with fluorescent tassels and a tiny top hat sporting a feather plume. From her belt hung a fuzzy skull totem, an homage to her voodoo heritage. Celia fanned out her brightly colored fortune-telling cards and let Mal pick one at random. It depicted the word *Journey* and an illustrated man at the end of a long winding path pointing toward the stars. Celia's eyes lit up. She pocketed her cards and flipped her sign to read THE FORTUNE TELLER IS OUT.

Mal put her arm around the spirited girl and led her down the alley toward her future.

Within minutes, Mal, Evie, Jay, and Carlos reunited in the center of Mal Court, followed closely by the boisterous parade of prospective students. They led the rambunctious throngs through a dank tunnel that exited into Bridge Plaza. The villain kids charged across the grungy plaza. The space looked out over the broken bridge that had once connected the Isle and Auradon. With VK Day upon them, there was now a promising new way for the Isle residents to reach the prosperous land. This euphoric crowd knew their four leaders were right: today it was good to be bad.

Mal, Evie, Carlos, and Jay climbed up the steps to a stone balcony overlooking the plaza. They eyed the rowdy mass of hopeful kids, who were waving their applications in the air and vying for the four former Isle kids' attention. "Who wants to go—you?" asked Mal, pointing at a girl in a moth-eaten red trench coat and purple tights.

Just then, she noticed Captain Hook's first mate, Smee, arriving late with his timid sons. They were twinned out in matching striped shirts, tortoiseshell glasses, and red stocking hats. Smee handed his scrawny offspring their applications, hugged them, and watched as his shy bespectacled sons handed them over. Jay collected the forms, handed them to Evie, and joined his friends to deliberate their difficult decision. This was going to be a tough one.

A little while later, the VKs broke from their huddle. The applications had been vetted; selections had been made. Mal scanned the crowd as she clutched one of the lucky applications in her right hand. She beamed with pride at Evie, clearly touched by her best friend's unwavering efforts. From that bold moment at Cotillion, when Evie first spoke to King Ben about bringing more VKs to Auradon, until this very second, when her thoughtful idea was coming to fruition, Evie never stopped fighting for her noble villain kids cause.

Shortly after Evie had first arrived at Auradon Prep, she resolved to make a clean break from the Isle and look only forward to the future. She didn't want to dwell on her Isle past, or even acknowledge it. Why spoil her beautiful Auradon life with thoughts of such depressing things? But everything shifted for Evie when she returned to the Isle to find Mal. Seeing all the wide-eyed villain offspring, just as miserable and desperate as she'd once been, Evie realized she couldn't just bury her connection to the Isle. Quite the opposite. She had to lean into her heritage and start helping others like herself. And Evie knew then just how to do it: by inviting additional Isle kids to Auradon and giving them the same life-changing opportunity King Ben had given her. Today she was doing just that.

Evie gazed out over the hordes of unkempt hooligans and beamed brightly. "I can't believe this day has finally arrived," she shouted. Her big wonderful dream for the Isle was coming true. She'd never felt so proud before.

The crowd of villain offspring cheered and howled for their blue-haired champion. "I honestly wish we could take you all with us. And someday very soon maybe we can," Evie said. Hope and determination crossed her face. The rowdy mob cheered loudly in support.

"Yeah, we're going to be back here so many times you'll get sick of us," promised Mal with a nod.

"So sick," repeated Evie with a sarcastic wave of her hand.

The frenzied crowd laughed with anticipation.

Evie flashed a smile at Jay, Carlos, and Mal and remembered the day King Ben had first invited the original Isle four to attend Auradon Prep. The limo, the chocolates, the awkward tour of the school grounds Doug gave them. The VKs had come a long way since they first arrived in Auradon. Now pillars of the Auradon community, Evie and her friends would share that dream-come-true chance with a new crop of kids from the Isle.

Poised as ever, Evie took a deep breath and asked: "Can I get a drumroll, please?" The mob was more than happy to oblige. They stamped and clopped their heavy boots and worn-down high-tops on the hard cement. The thundering result echoed through the plaza like a drumroll.

Evie looked down at her red gloves with heart-shaped cutouts and the application she clenched in her hands. "First, I would like to begin with the grand-daughter of Lady Tremaine, daughter of Drizella, my sweet, sweet friend, my Dizzy." Evie was thrilled to make the invitation public at last. She could think of no one more deserving of a fresh start in Auradon than the sprightly girl who forged chic fashion-forward accessories out of lousy dumpster junk.

Dizzy shrieked with delight upon hearing her name. She squealed so loudly her shouts of joy were heard way on the other side of Goblin Wharf. Goblins hated joy. But Dizzy's glee could not be contained. She was headed to Auradon with Evie. *Best. Day. Ever.* Dizzy spun with delight, then skipped to meet Evie on the balcony, her rainbow tulle skirt flouncing as she went.

All eyes turned to Carlos, who stepped forward to name the second lucky VK. "Next is son of Smee," said Carlos. "C'mon, Squeaky!"

Squeaky, wide-eyed and silent, looked at his dad for reassurance. Smee gently nudged the boy toward Carlos, who greeted him with a warm hug. Squeaky squished up his face, tugged at his stained shirt, and, still unsure, looked longingly toward the crowd at his twin brother, Squirmy. The two had never spent a day apart. Now there'd be an ocean between them. Was Auradon really worth it?

But Jay quickly stepped in and put Squeaky's fears to rest. "And no way we're splitting up the twins . . . so get over here, Squirmy, come on!" he announced. Jay knelt down to Squirmy's height, hoping to put the shy boy at ease. "Bring it in, buddy."

Squeaky broke into a smile as his brother, Squirmy, ran forward. It was impossible to tell which brother was more relieved about the reunion. It was also impossible to tell which brother was which. That was exactly the way Smee's introverted sons liked it.

Mal stepped forward to reveal the final name. The antsy Isle kids all leaned in anxiously, each one desperately hoping to hear his or her own name called.

"And last, but certainly not least . . . we all picked this girl, because we all agreed that she could use a little bit of Fairy Godmother's goodness class," said Mal, thinking back to the class she had loathed the most during her first days in Auradon. "Give it on up for Dr. Facilier's daughter, Celia."

As soon as she heard her name, Celia busted out in a brash touchdown victory dance. "I'm bad," she said, and showboated for the crowd. She trotted up to Mal, brazenly slapping high fives to her friends along the way.

Mal, Evie, Carlos, and Jay put their arms around the newly selected class. Mal and her friends wished they could whisk the kids away to Auradon that very minute, but it was against the agreed-upon protocol. The future students would spend a week packing their belongings and saying so long to their villainous families before heading off to their fresh start across the bay.

"We'll be back for you next week," Carlos assured them.

"So pack your stuff," instructed Jay, employing the same authoritative tone he used when acting as tourney team captain. "Your *own* stuff," he added quickly, knowing all too well the wily pilfering ways of young Isle thieves.

Mal, Evie, Jay, and Carlos smiled at the crowd, relishing the events of VK Day. They'd actually done it! They'd paved the way and opened the door for more VKs to make a new home in Auradon.

"Where are we going?" shouted Mal and Evie, wanting to get the new kids psyched up.

"We're going to Auradon," yelled Dizzy, Celia, Squeaky, and Squirmy in unison. They were definitely psyched.

And so it began.

CHAPTER THREE

ALL'S QUIET ON THE AURADON FRONT, WHICH DOESN'T FEEL RIGHT. AS IF UMA'S NOT JUST WAITING UNDER THE SEA FOR HER CHANCE TO POUNCE. OR JUMP. OR WHATEVER IT IS GIANT OCTOPUSES DO.

One week later, Mal stood guard by herself on Auradon Prep's back balcony, looking every bit the fierce protector in a dragon-patterned dress and dragon-wing epaulets. The school's blue-and-yellow flags flapped in the wind above her as she took in the morning air. The castle-like building's pale stone bricks were sturdy beneath her feet, but Mal still felt uneasy. Auradon could never be truly safe while Ursula's daughter, Uma, was still out there.

Mal scanned the vast horizon for signs of Uma. As far as Mal could see, the spectacular Auradon coastline lay quiet and peaceful, all rolling green hills and sparkling blue seas. But beyond the calm sea hunched the Isle of the Lost. Its magical, isolating barrier flickered and shimmered in the morning sun, the Isle's dangerous population imprisoned behind it.

Today's the big day, Mal thought. It was time to pick up the new VKs. She smiled to herself with pride. Mal, daughter of Auradon's most-hated villain, spawn of the Isle's mistress of evil, had passed all her senior classes (without the help of magic) and graduated from Auradon Prep. And her best friend, Evie, had finished at the top of their elite prep school class. They were truly Auradon girls now.

Mal shook her head and refocused on her critical task. She had to be sure Uma wasn't going to mess things up and slip her angry octopus self into Mal's peaceful life in Auradon. Mal shivered and recalled Uma's disturbing transformation at Cotillion, from a wicked leader of rapscallion pirates into an eight-legged aqua-beast. No one had seen or heard from Uma since. Mal's top priority was keeping Auradon a safe place for all the people she loved.

Deep in thought, Mal failed to notice that her boyfriend, King Ben, had walked up behind her on the balcony. The handsome royal put his arms gently around Mal's waist and surprised her with a giant hug. Romantic surprises were one of Ben's specialties. He was always making grand, unexpected gestures, like planning picnics by the Enchanted Lake or commissioning a personalized stained-glass window of him and Mal for Cotillion. Ben got so much pleasure out of seeing Mal's joyful and shocked reactions to his surprises. This time was no different.

Mal jumped, whirled around, and greeted her dreamy boyfriend with a loving smile.

"Not a tentacle in sight," Mal declared, taking Ben's strong hand in hers.

"I believe if Uma was up to something, we'd know by now," said Ben reassuringly. The king looked sharp and self-assured in his cobalt blue suit with its yellow pocket square. His honey-brown hair shifted across his forehead as he scanned the water.

"I know how villains think, and I don't trust her as far as I can throw her. She's going to wait until our guard is down and then strike," Mal said, looking thoughtful as she mulled over potential evil plots in her head. "I really wish I had time to do a dragon flyover, 'cuz I could go much higher."

Ever since Mal's brilliant Cotillion metamorphosis into a magnificent fire-breathing dragon, she'd been soaring over Auradon on a daily basis and safeguarding the kingdom from above. Because her dragon's-eye view provided an unrivaled perspective, Mal felt it was her personal responsibility to protect Auradon from harm.

"Well, you can't be everywhere at once," said Ben, concerned that Mal was taking on too much. He loved her passion for Auradon's safety, but the security of the country didn't rest on Mal's shoulders alone, even if she thought otherwise. Ben wished Mal knew how to lean more on others for help. She wasn't on the Isle anymore; she didn't have to do everything alone. Ben did his best to help her see that.

"Besides, I've got your back." He gestured above to dozens of gallant royal guards positioned on the school's high parapet, their telescopes carefully arranged to cover every direction.

Then, remembering why he'd come to get Mal, Ben threw his arm around her. "Now come on, everybody's waiting for us," he reminded her. Ben couldn't wait to welcome the new batch of Isle kids to his kingdom.

With Mal and her friends, Ben had witnessed first-hand how an invitation to Auradon Prep changed not just the lives of the VKs who came over, but the lives of everyone they met as well—including himself. Ben could never have predicted that his groundbreaking proclamation for Auradon Prep's integration would lead to his meeting the love of his life. But the wise leader *had* foreseen that given the right education and resources, villain kids could change. Children raised by evil parents could choose to be good. Mal, Evie, Jay, and Carlos had. If only Uma had made the same choice. He had thought more of her. Instead, they all nervously awaited her return. Especially Mal.

"Wait, you're getting more guards?" Mal asked, searching for reassurance in Ben's eyes.

"I'm getting more guards," he replied. He took both of her hands in his. "Now breathe."

Mal leaned back and took a deep cleansing breath.

"C'mon," Ben said. He wrapped his arm around her playfully as they crossed the balcony to exit.

"Okay." Mal leaned into him, thankful to have him by her side.

CHAPTER FOUR

I CAN'T BELIEVE HOW MANY PEOPLE ARE HERE JUST TO GREET THE NEW VKS. THE ONLY GREETING PARTY WE GOT WAS FAIRY GODMOTHER, WHO NERVOUSLY REMINDED US ABOUT CURFEW, AND AUDREY, WHO KEPT CALLING BEN "BENNY BOO." MAYBE THINGS REALLY HAVE CHANGED.

Pastel-clad students, teachers, and parents gathered eagerly on Auradon Prep's front lawn to greet the school's newest Isle additions. Throngs of curious Auradonians had flocked to the event and were milling about the well-groomed gardens, converging under the King Beast statue and clustering on the school steps. They were all beyond excited to welcome the second wave of villain students to their side of the sea.

The Auradon Knights marching band, wearing

snappy blue-and-gold uniforms, blasted out a toe-tapping number as the school's cheer squad shook their pom-poms and rallied the growing crowd. Ben's parents, Beast and Belle, mingled among the crowd, looking as proud as ever of their son and his efforts to rule the kingdom with kindness. The royal couple smiled at each other, noting all the electrified citizens who were waving homemade WELCOME ALL posters, flying painted REUNITE banners, and holding cheery flower bouquets.

Queen Leah and her granddaughter, Audrey, daughter of Sleeping Beauty, stood near a row of meticulously trimmed hedges. The two looked on with considerably less enthusiasm than most. Audrey's mouth formed a serious line, and her brown eyes were unsmiling. She pulled at her long ash-brown hair—which was newly streaked with pink and blue—straightened her pink leather ensemble, and frowned at all the hoopla. Auradon Prep did not need more evil-offspring students. The first four had been more than enough for her taste.

The rest of Auradon, however, felt differently.

A giant video monitor was set up atop the school's battlements to carry a real-time feed of the Isle's barrier opening. WELCOME TO OUR NEW VKS blazed across its screen. A formal royal guard detail stood in their pressed gold uniforms around the lawn. The king's stretch limo, now painted purple in Mal's honor, sat parked and ready to go in the circular driveway. In a few moments it would be crossing the barrier to pick up the four new VKs.

Many Auradon students, like Fairy Godmother's daughter, Jane, were eager to befriend their new villain classmates. Jane held tightly to Carlos's arm as he told her all about the twins. She couldn't wait to meet them.

Doug, son of Dopey, was equally enthusiastic. He waited next to Evie in his full band uniform—complete with brass buttons and a tall gold hat— excited to finally welcome the famous Dizzy. Evie had shared many stories about her precious Isle friend. Evie laughed with delight, flirtatiously took Doug's arm, then noticed something out of the corner of her eye. "Here they come," she gasped. Doug and Evie shared knowing looks filled with happy anticipation. Then Doug took hold of his drum major baton and started to lead the band in an upbeat tune.

Mal and Ben made their grand entrance into the packed festivities. Mal surveyed the bustling celebratory scene, quite pleased to see the newest VKs would be greeted with more excitement and fanfare than she and her friends had been when they'd first arrived. She was amazed by how things in Auradon had truly changed.

Ben adjusted his golden crown, which bore the Beast family crest, and stepped in front of the crowd to speak. Mal moved to join her crew, but Fairy Godmother blocked her path. "Oooh, stay," said Fairy Godmother, looking proper as always in a conservative powder-blue dress.

"Stay here?" asked Mal, taking her place by Ben's side on the stage. The couple waved to the jubilant crowd. Mal, who had once found the royal wave rather awkward, now performed it like a pro.

"Bibbidi-bobbidi, one two, one two. Can everybody hear me?" asked Fairy Godmother, testing the microphone. "Ben," she said pointedly, and passed him the golden mic.

"Thank you, Fairy Godmother," said the king. Then he broke out one of his trademark warm smiles that put everyone at ease. Ben had really come into his own as the leader of the country. His approval ratings were off the chart.

"What's up, Auradon?" the king belted with rock-star style. "Thank you, thank you so much for coming out to welcome our new arrivals. They'll be here soon." His first official act as king had been inviting the children of Auradon's sworn enemies to live among them. At the time, the royal proclamation had been controversial to say the least. But Ben's courage, conviction, and risk paid off, and now all the citizens of Auradon were cheering on the arrival of more VKs.

Well, most of the citizens. Queen Leah, clearly displeased, pulled nervously at the strand of pearls around her wrist, leaned over to Audrey, and whispered, "Not like we had a choice." Audrey nodded back, unsmiling.

"It worked out pretty well with the first four," Ben mused to the crowd.

"Especially for you," Chad, the preppy son of Cinderella and Prince Charming, shouted back. His blond curls shook as he laughed at his own clever joke.

"Yeah. Real funny," said Audrey. She snapped her fingers and Chad cowered in obedience.

Ben gazed out at his subjects, then turned to face Mal and focused only on her. "Mal," he said, smiling at his girlfriend, "this is the exact spot where we first met not so long ago."

Doug suddenly removed his marching band hat. His shoulder-length blond hair sprang free. Evie handed him a guitar and grinned conspiratorially. Doug stepped forward, cleared his throat, and began strumming an acoustic version of "Did I Mention." It was the song Ben had serenaded Mal with when he first declared his love to her in a very public way after a tourney victory.

Ben spoke softly into the mic, addressing Mal. "I feel like I've known you my whole life. Did I mention I'm in love with you?"

Ben spoke from his heart as he told Mal that he never thought love like this would happen to a guy like him. Then he bent down on one knee.

Mal gasped audibly.

Ben held out a little blue box. Inside was a spectacular one-of-a-kind vintage-style ring with an enormous purple stone encased in a dragon design. It was by far Ben's most romantic surprise for Mal yet. "It's you and me, Mal. It's you and me forever. Will you marry me? Will you wear the crown and be my queen?"

But before Mal could respond, Audrey blurted out, "No!" She couldn't stop herself. The people who stood around her glared at the interruption.

"Yes. *Yes!*" exploded Mal, who, fortunately, hadn't heard Audrey. Happiness danced across her face. She couldn't believe she was getting married to Ben! The Auradon palace bells pealed loudly as Ben slipped the ring on Mal's finger, stood up, and embraced her. The couple kissed—a real True Love's Kiss—as if they were the only two people in the world.

The crowd instantly erupted in wild applause as a cannon released a sea of bubbles into the air.

Evie, Belle, and Fairy Godmother all had tears in their eyes. Carlos, who'd thrown on Doug's band hat, chest-bumped Beast, then turned to find Jay. The two pals clapped and pumped their fists, ecstatic for their friends. Dozens of onlookers flipped their DIY welcome signs to reveal sweet congratulatory messages like *Queen Mal*, *Happily Ever After*, and *True Love, Mal!*

Doug and Evie high-fived each other for their clever signage and exceptional teamwork. They really did work well together. Doug took in the massive scale of Ben's romantic gesture and shrugged sheepishly. "It makes our movie nights seem a little tame," he said humbly.

In contrast to Ben and Mal's relationship, Evie and Doug's flirtship was progressing at a measured pace. Not that they didn't spend time together or make each other happy. But there was one big bridge they hadn't crossed yet.

Evie looked at Doug tenderly and full of appreciation. "I love yo—our movie nights." She seemed to have wanted to say something else, but just smiled instead.

"Me too," said Doug. He smiled back awkwardly.

"Yeah," said Evie, turning away quickly. Why couldn't she say what she felt? She was happy to wear an oversized heart pendant around her neck, but she wasn't one to wear her real heart on her sleeve.

Audrey, surrounded by the colossal celebration of love, felt crushed under the weight of utter devastation and raw heartache from losing Ben for good. Hearing that stupid song again only made things worse. Queen Leah narrowed her eyes with fury at her disappointing granddaughter, her pink ruffled collar framing the dour frown on her face. "A lifetime of plans. Gone," she said. "Our family status. Gone. You were supposed to be his queen and you let him slip through your fingers. Your mother could hold on to a prince in her sleep."

Audrey winced and tried to hold back the tears she felt coming. She swallowed the cold lump that had formed in her throat. "Don't you think I feel bad enough already, Grammy?"

A squad of girls stood next to them, delighting loudly in the sheer romance of Ben's proposal and chatting giddily about it. "Ben and Mal are the best," said one. "I'm so excited for Mal to be our queen," said another.

Audrey turned on them angrily. "You'd really rather have a VK on the throne than me?" she asked angrily. "What is wrong with you people?"

The girls rolled their eyes, laughed among themselves, and took their happiness elsewhere. But it didn't matter. Everywhere Audrey looked, all of Auradon seemed to be rejoicing over Mal and Ben's engagement. "What is wrong with everybody?" she fumed.

She watched with hurt-filled eyes as Evie ran to Mal and hugged her tightly. "Wait, did you know?" Mal, clearly still shocked, asked Evie.

"Everything," replied an overjoyed Evie. She couldn't have been happier for Mal or thought of a single person who would make a better queen. "You're really going to rock that crown," Evie added, running her hand along Mal's long purple strands.

Then Evie turned to more important business. "I've done about a thousand sketches of your wedding dress. And Belle's already planning an engagement party for next week," she said, enamored with the idea of all the fun wedding planning that lay ahead.

Mal tilted her head and laughed. "Then it's a really good thing that I said yes."

Belle and Beast, all smiles, joined them. "Hugs, hi," Beast proclaimed, and swallowed up Mal in a giant father-in-law-to-be bear hug.

"Hugs, hi," replied Mal, glowing and at home with the royal family.

"I finally get a daughter," said Belle, her face filled with sheer joy.

"I love you, Belle," said Mal. And she meant it.

I love you, too, mouthed Belle in return.

Mal hugged them both. She was grateful to be joining a family who loved and supported one another.

Teeming with happiness, Ben looked at the family scene and turned toward Fairy Godmother. "Thank you so much for your help, Fairy Godmother. I think she liked it," he said. He glanced back at Mal and felt like the luckiest guy in the world.

"Bibbidi-bobbidi you betcha," said a very pleased Fairy Godmother.

No sooner had Fairy Godmother congratulated Ben with a warm pat on the back and hurried off than Evie, Carlos, and Jay bounded to Mal with goofy, exaggerated steps. Jay bowed elaborately in Mal's direction and spoke, his voice syrupy with sarcasm: "All bow to Your Royal Majesty."

Evie curtsied with overblown reverence.

Carlos followed suit. "Your Royal Purpleness," he said between stifled laughs.

"Silence, annoying peasants," Mal told them, shooing away her friends with feigned disinterest.

"As you wish, my liege," said Jay, who rose from his ridiculous prostrate pose.

"Your Crankiness," added Carlos. The boys continued to crack themselves up as they bowed and scraped away, happy that although Mal was the future queen of Auradon, at heart she'd always be their goofy friend.

Mal turned to find Audrey staring at her with disdain. Her smile immediately faded; this couldn't be good.

"Congratulations. You won him fair and square," said Audrey. Then she cocked her head. "Oh, wait, no you didn't. You spelled Ben to destroy all of Auradon. Touching story for the grandkids," she sneered.

"Okay. Let's do this," said Ben, who stood nearby, unaware of Audrey's comment. He glanced at his watch, then fist-bumped Jay and Carlos with new focus. They were expected elsewhere. The king was clearly in good spirits and ready to head to the Isle to pick up Dizzy, Celia, Squeaky, and Squirmy.

Mal flashed a fake grin at Audrey. "Speaking of kids, we have some kids waiting on us. So if you'll excuse me . . ." she said, leaving a stony Audrey behind.

With a pained expression, Audrey watched as the royal attendants opened the limo doors for King Ben, Mal, Evie, and Carlos while Jay jumped effortlessly into the driver's seat. The limo's custom license plate now read MAL, in honor of the queen-to-be.

CHAPTER FIVE

WHAT IN THE HADES?

A crowd of Isle kids and has-been villains stared at the shiny purple limo in awe. Its sparkling finish stood out against the dingy film that seemed to cover everything on the Isle.

Smee, wearing a striped shirt and a red cap, hugged his two mini-mes and gave them each a quick kiss on the head.

"All right, boys, let's hit the road," Jay said enthusiastically, throwing his arm around an anxious Squeaky, who wore one red glove on his right hand.

"You're gonna see him soon, okay?" Carlos reassured a fearful Squirmy, who wore one red glove on his left hand. "C'mon," he added gently, and walked Squirmy toward the car. Carlos, who'd been filled with trepidation himself during his first trip to Auradon, empathized with the twins. But he knew the sweet boys would flourish in their new environment. And he would be there to look after them.

In contrast to the nervous brothers, Dizzy was ecstatic about traveling to Auradon. She'd always dreamed of living in the magical land and couldn't kick-start her new adventure fast enough. "Do you have everything?" asked her grandmother Lady Tremaine, looking grim as usual in her high-collared crimson dress. Her hair, piled in a colossal pompadour, only added to the wicked grandmother's stern air.

"Yes, I have everything!" exclaimed Dizzy. Her hair was fastened in two topknots secured with a turquoise flower barrette she'd made herself. She couldn't wait to create her signature accessories out of all the rich materials she'd find across the bay.

"Are you sure?" asked Lady Tremaine. Her voice sounded cold.

"I'm sure, Granny."

Lady Tremaine raised her eyebrow questioningly. "Oh, really?" She held up a small object.

"My glue gun!" gushed Dizzy. She couldn't believe she'd almost forgotten her prized crafting tool.

"I don't know what you're going to do without me," remarked her grandmother, feigning indifference.

Dizzy held her hands to her chest and replied sincerely, "I'll miss you."

"Go on, go on," said Lady Tremaine. She tugged at her brooch, fighting hard not to show emotion.

Evie, who'd been watching the touching exchange, gave Dizzy an encouraging wink. Dizzy threw her arms wide open and surprised her granny with an enormous heartfelt hug. Then Dizzy skipped with glee to join the others leaving for Auradon Prep.

Last to approach the car was Celia, dressed in a wild multicolored skirt and jacket and flanked by Ben and Mal. "Let me get this off of you," Mal offered, reaching for Celia's backpack. But Dr. Facilier's plucky, independent daughter wanted no help. She flung her backpack into the trunk with attitude.

"Oh," Mal said, laughing.

"Okay, let's go and do—" King Ben stopped mid-sentence as Celia strutted away toward the limo without acknowledging him. "Let's do this," he finished, sharing a laugh with Mal. They could tell Celia was going to be a handful.

With everyone squished tightly in the vehicle and buckled in, Jay climbed into the driver's seat and revved the engine. He grinned devilishly as he steered the limo down the narrow streets and railed it around the neighborhood's craggy corners. He rocketed the royal car toward the enchanted bridge that would magically appear to connect the dismal Isle of the Lost with the dazzling United States of Auradon.

Inside the limo, the VKs buzzed with anticipation. It was the first time any of the younger four had been in a car, and it showed. There were so many shiny buttons to press and switches to pull. Life in Auradon was already more fascinating than life on the Isle, and they hadn't even left yet.

The car was just the start of all the exciting new things that awaited the VKs in Auradon. Evie patted

Dizzy's knee encouragingly. "So as soon as you get to Auradon, you have to try ice cream," said Evie, whose long blue hair hung straight and shiny that morning.

"And go swimming!" Dizzy said enthusiastically.

"I can take you to the Enchanted Lake," said Evie. They were going to have so much fun together. Evie had made a long list of things she couldn't wait to introduce Dizzy to—ballet, volleyball, the periodic table. For Evie, the only thing better than living in Auradon was getting to share it with others.

Dizzy nodded in enthusiastic agreement. "I can't believe that I get to live with you in your very own castle!" she exclaimed.

"It's just a starter castle," Evie said, blushing. But she was proud of herself; she'd bought the charming home with the profits from her wildly successful fashion line.

Squirmy sat shotgun and nervously clutched at Jay's firm bicep with every wild turn. As Jay pried the youngster's tightly clenched fingers from his arm, he noticed the kid's strength. "Great grip," Jay said. "You play any sports?"

In the limo's back seat, Carlos handed Squeaky an enormous chocolate peanut butter cup. "Here, go on. Trust me on this," Carlos told him, recalling his first delicious taste of chocolate in that very limo on his initial trip across the bridge. He was eager to watch someone else enjoy it for the first time. Squeaky eyed the sweet object suspiciously, then took a bite. His reaction was nothing short of euphoric, which was exactly what Carlos had counted on. He laughed when Squeaky quickly took a second bite. "I know," said Carlos, putting his arm around Squeaky's shoulder. "Dig in, dig in."

Celia, who seemed not to have a care in the world, fanned out her fortune cards in her hand and attempted to read King Ben's fortune. "You're going to be a wise and brave king," she predicted grandly.

"He already is," said Mal.

"See? The cards never lie," Celia mused, then held out her palm to Ben, demanding payment.

Flustered, Ben fished for a bill from his wallet to give to the fortune-telling VK. She looked thrilled to receive such generous payment.

Mal had no doubt that Celia was going to require a little extra work.

At Auradon Prep, the crowd watched the video screen's live feed with mounting suspense. Right before their eyes, the magical barrier that separated Auradon and the Isle began to open. It was an incredible sight. But not everyone was impressed.

"The only reason they should be opening that barrier is to be putting Uma back in, not letting more villains out," scoffed Queen Leah with a disapproving scowl.

On the Isle of the Lost, a riotous mass congregated on Bridge Plaza, in part to bid farewell to the four chosen students, but mostly to witness with their own eyes the normally impassable barrier open. It had been a long time since any of them had seen magic, which had been rendered impossible on the Isle of the Lost.

With the barrier flickering open, the regal limo started to make its way through. Jay gripped the wheel and drove with focus as the crowd pointed and snarled. The disgruntled onlookers seemed ready to cause serious trouble. Jay resolved to get the limo across safely, without any hitchhiking thieves or uninvited passengers.

Before Jay could finish that thought, a rugged scoundrel with faded rock-star good looks, spiked blue hair, and hollow, sunken eyes forcefully pushed and elbowed his way to the front of the raucous crowd. The crowd scurried aside in fear as he barged to the front and beelined for the bridge. He noticed the barrier was starting to close and broke into a fast run.

Just as the barrier was about to finish closing, Evie turned to watch the unfolding chaos through the car's back window. She couldn't help feeling a tinge of disappointment. The day had been going so smoothly; it was just like a villain to ruin it. Evie immediately recognized the blue-haired interloper.

"It's Hades!" she warned, pointing at the rebel dressed in his signature gray chiton, gray T-shirt, and studded leather coat etched with blue flames. "Stop the car. He's trying to escape."

Mal twisted around and gasped with alarm. Hades was no ordinary villain. As the great god of the Underworld and vicious collector of souls, Hades ranked with Mal's mother, Maleficent, at the top of the evil-o-meter. Mal knew the havoc he could wreak if he escaped to Auradon City.

The immortal villain strode furiously toward the rapidly closing barrier. After years of suffering on the Isle, he would not miss his fleeting chance at freedom. With a keen eye, he noticed a sliver-sized crack that remained open in the barrier. The small gap was all he needed. Hades thrust his mighty hands through the breach and strained to widen it.

The royal vehicle screeched to a violent halt mid-bridge. Within seconds, Mal leapt from the limo, telling herself it was her duty to keep Auradon safe. She would not let Hades pass. Evie, Jay, Carlos, and Ben jumped out of the limo as well, while the younger kids craned their necks to watch the action from the safety of the back seat. Their eyes were glued on Hades as he struggled with the closing barrier.

"I am a god," he bellowed. "I don't belong here." Hades's sculpted muscles bulged with effort. Summoning every bit of his colossal strength, he pried open the barrier just wide enough to push his right fist through it. Wicked glee flooded his face as he opened his tightly clenched hand to reveal a small blue ember. The magical ember, which for decades had remained dull and dormant on the Isle, came to life the second it hit Auradon's air. The light from the ember made his eyes glow dangerously.

With his hands and arms completely through the barrier, Hades squeezed his head and shoulders through next. Like the ember before it, Hades's spiked hair burst into scorching blue and white flames the instant it crossed into Auradon. After years of being held in abeyance, Hades's almighty magic surged through him. He cackled darkly, then aimed the blazing blue ember in his hand directly at Mal's friends. It released a magical hot blue laser beam in their direction. Ben, Jay, and Carlos were struck to the ground by the powerful blue force while Evie backed away toward the limo. Hades forged toward them.

"No!" screamed Mal. She would not let Hades harm those she treasured most. Her angry eyes flashed bright green and she vanished in a cloud of swirling purple smoke. In a glimmer, Mal reemerged as a glorious purple dragon with opalescent scales, a spiky barbed tail, two curved horns, and an enormous and intimidating wingspan.

Dragon Mal spread her exquisite wings and swooped down on Hades. He was undaunted. To someone who had seen every monstrous creature imaginable in the Underworld, a dragon was nothing to fear. In fact, after years of Isle idleness, the diabolical villain welcomed the fight. Hades snarled, raised his right arm, and hurled his crackling ember at Mal. The sizzling stone released a piercing blue laser light that locked on to Dragon Mal and began to drain her awesome power.

That was new. Dragon Mal shook her head in disbelief. How was he doing that? Severely weakened, she dropped lower and lower in the sky.

Jay, Carlos, and Ben exchanged frightened looks. The teens had heard about Hades's incomparable magic, but until that day, it'd been just another fright-time story parents told their kids before bed. Now they watched in terror as Hades easily overpowered their friend.

At Auradon Prep, the crowd of gathered students and onlookers gasped and screamed, their eyes glued to the terrifying sight on the screen. They watched in shock as Mal, incapacitated, flapped helplessly toward the ground.

Fairy Godmother valiantly vaulted onto the platform, grabbed the mic, and attempted to take swift control of the situation. "Do not panic, okay? Nobody needs to panic!"

Unlike the others, Audrey seemed to revel in the developing turmoil. "There's your precious queen," she snarled, pointing toward a depleted Mal on the live feed. "She can't even protect us."

As if on cue, Hades's sinister face and monstrous flaming hair filled the screen threateningly. Even Fairy Godmother was spooked. She took one look at the screen and screamed. "Okay, we're panicking. Bibbidi-bobbidi run!" she shrieked, and bounded away. Terrified students followed the headmistress's example, becoming hysterical and scattering hastily.

Back on the Isle, Jay watched the battle with grave concern. "C'mon, Mal, blast him," he bellowed. His encouragement gave Mal the extra boost of confidence she needed.

With her final burst of energy, Dragon Mal reared back, opened her jaw wide, and prepared to release fiery havoc on Hades. But to her and everyone else's surprise, instead of unleashing a fireball, the dragon exhaled mightily and hit Hades with a forceful gust of air, which blew out his burning hair and extinguished his blazing ember. Hades tumbled back to the Isle with a thud. The magical barrier immediately shut and resealed, recondemning Hades to Isle imprisonment.

Dizzy, Squeaky, Squirmy, and Celia hopped out of the limo. Battle-worn, Dragon Mal landed on the limo roof and morphed back into an everyday tough-as-nails teenage girl, although a little singed. And a lot more concerned.

Evie and Ben ran to Mal and helped her down. They were legitimately terrified for their friend. In all the years Evie had known Mal, she had never seen Mal come so close to defeat. "Hey, are you okay?" asked Evie as she patted down Mal's charred dress hem.

Mal caught her breath. Then, with an uneasy feeling in her chest, she opened up to her friends. "No, he was draining all my magic with his ember. And I felt all of my powers slipping away." A shiver ran through Mal as she relived the moment.

Evie had never seen Mal that shaken; she was clearly rattled to her bones. Unsure of how to help, Evie tried to be there for her friend. "It's okay, he's back where he belongs," she said.

"Yeah, for now," said Mal. She stared back at the Isle and frowned.

"We should go," whispered Jay.

"Okay," agreed Mal. As her friends helped her back into the car, Mal leaned on them for physical and emotional support. She would need them more than ever now.

CHAPTER SIX

I DID NOT TAKE THAT GIRL FOR EVIL. I MEAN, SHE ALWAYS WORE SO MUCH PINK.

Audrey sat on her queen-size bed and sketched furiously in a rose-colored journal trimmed with gold scrolling. Dressed in a beaded bodysuit with pink leather pants and an open leather duster, pink ankle boots, pink feather earrings, and a sweet bluebird charm necklace, Audrey screamed *goody-goody*. As did everything about her dorm room, with its pink curtains, pink bedding, and pink marble fireplace. A glinting crystal chandelier hung from the ceiling. Several handsomely framed portraits of Audrey and Ben through the years received prime placement on the fireplace mantel. In one particularly sweet photo, a cherubic five-year-old Audrey was seated on a miniature gold throne next to Prince Ben, who wore a teensy-tiny Auradon crown and held out a matching one toward Audrey. It was an adorable depiction of their destined royal future together.

Audrey looked up from her journal and scowled at the old photo, a sharp reminder of what was never to be. She'd followed all the rules and waited patiently, but when the time finally came, Ben chose Mal. A villain! Audrey's heart shattered all over again at the thought of his cruel rejection. She returned her attention to her journal and attacked the page with angry strokes of the pencil. The sketch she drew was haunting: a majestic portrait of herself as Auradon's queen, wearing a resplendent gold-and-sapphire crown atop her head. Audrey's brown eyes filled with tears. She looked at her sketch and wondered, *What happened to my happy ending?*

She hurled her journal across the room and strode to her dorm room door, grabbing a fireplace poker on her way out. Her face was set with resolution. If she couldn't be Ben's queen, then she'd show

Auradon. Ben wanted a villain. Well, he'd get one. Mal wasn't the only one who could succeed at breaking and entering.

A CLOSED sign hung on the wrought iron doors of the Auradon Museum of Cultural History. Behind it a single guard slept obliviously at his post. Audrey snuck across the silent museum lobby, which held her mother's spinning wheel. She crept past a glass case displaying the Genie of Agrabah's lamp and another exhibiting Cinderella's glass slipper, then stood thoughtfully in front of the security console. Without a sound, she deftly turned knobs and pushed buttons, which shut off alerts and silenced alarms. Then she swiftly climbed the steep foyer stairs, proud of her first successful foray into crime. See? There was nothing to this being-evil thing.

On the second floor, Audrey crept down a dimly lit hallway and tiptoed into the museum's Room of Crowns. It was a guilded gallery that showcased the glorious tiaras and crowns of the queens and kings of fairy tales past. When Audrey was a young girl, the regal room had been her happy place. Tonight, she walked by the dazzling tiaras of everyday royals and headed straight to the far end of the room. A sign read *Crown of the Queen of Auradon*. She pulled back the blue velvet curtain and bounded up the few steps to a lit glass case that held the breathtaking crown. The gem-covered object of beauty was the same magnificent two-tiered gold, diamond, and sapphire crown Audrey had drawn herself wearing. In accordance with kingdom tradition, the crown was meant to sit on the head of King Ben's chosen queen— which, Audrey fumed, was supposed to be her. Oh, how she coveted the stunning crown and everything it represented. She was not about to sit by and let the most precious heirloom in the land be worn by that dreadful daughter of Maleficent. She'd sooner steal the beloved crown than let that happen. Audrey was tired of playing nice. "Your nightmare's my dream," she said as if speaking to the people of Auradon. With anger and hurt boiling in her blood, Audrey hoisted the iron poker in the air and smashed the glass case.

At the sound of the shattered glass, something evil awoke down the hall in the museum's Room of the Dark Arts. As if roused by Audrey's villainous intentions, Maleficent's scepter, which had sat dormant on a spotlighted pedestal for years, began to pulse with an eerie green light. There was something ominous and wicked about its glow.

Meanwhile, Audrey stood in the Room of Crowns among the scattered shards of glass, with the iron poker at her feet. She grabbed the majestic sapphire-laden crown from the case and raised it defiantly above her head.

Suddenly, a red velvet curtain flapped open across the room. A green-tinged light cascaded in from a hidden chamber behind it. Audrey, mesmerized by the sinister light, clutched the prized crown in her manicured hand. She glided down the steps and followed the mysterious beacon. In all her years of school field trips and family outings to the museum, Audrey had never set foot in the Room of the Dark Arts. And now it beckoned her. The hypnotic glow emanated from Maleficent's scepter. Audrey floated to the forbidden object, drawn to its promise of unlimited power and sweet revenge. In the presence of the scepter, Audrey changed her mind. The night was no longer about the mere theft of the bejeweled crown. The scepter had opened Audrey's eyes to the possibility of much more than that. "I want what I deserve. I want to rule the world," Audrey said aloud.

An excellent student, Audrey knew the museum housed only one object powerful enough to assist in that goal, and that artifact had once belonged to Mal's mom. Now it would belong to her. How fitting.

Her gaze darted about the Room of the Dark Arts and stopped on a straw basket lined with a red-and-white gingham napkin and filled with a dozen of Evil Queen's poisoned apples. With a quick sweep of her arm, Audrey cleared the basket from its pedestal and set down the bejeweled crown in its place. She'd take the scepter instead. She strode toward Maleficent's staff, her gait powered by awe and hunger, but then she paused, turned around, and returned to retrieve the crown. She didn't have to choose between the queen's crown and the deadly scepter. Ben wanted a true villain? Well, a true villain would steal both. So she did. Audrey placed the queen's crown regally on her own head. "I am the queen and my reign will be endless."

With her self-coronation complete, Queen Audrey yanked the pulsing scepter off its stand. The orb changed at her touch, instantly turning a more menacing shade of green. Audrey's eyes widened as the potent evil force swept through her body, transforming the prissy pink princess into a dark, dangerous sorceress.

Audrey's evil new look was heart-stopping. Her pale, anemic hair had turned a rich magenta ombré, flowing from deep rose at the roots to midnight blue at the tips. Her demure pastel pink outfit was no more. In its place, she wore a wicked getup of black-and-blush fitted leather pants and a tea-length duster with alarming black feather accents. Her necklace now featured two charms, a bright bluebird and a dark black raven. Audrey looked like a warrior enchantress—gorgeous and menacing and scary.

A maniacal look washed over Audrey's pretty face as she decided to take Maleficent's scepter for a test run. She raised the staff aloft and unleashed its power on the crystal chandelier above. The fixture shattered in a menacing cascade of glass and light. Audrey's nefarious laugh echoed throughout the museum. Being an evil queen was going to be fun.

CHAPTER SEVEN

LIFE WAS SO MUCH SIMPLER ON THE ISLE, WHEN MY ONLY TOUGH DECISION WAS WHAT TO STEAL FOR BREAKFAST.

Ben's picturesque palace was built from gleaming white masonry and sat perched on a noble hilltop overlooking the rocky bay. It featured round turrets, tall regal spires, and a wide rampart that encircled the entire property. The countless palace wings included an armory, a stable, a formal conference room, a ballroom, a carriage house, and, because he was such a thoughtful son, suites for both of his parents.

Belle's parlor was painted a sunny buttercup yellow with white trim. The cheery room was filled with cushy floral couches, fresh flower arrangements, and a baby grand piano. King Ben and Mal stood in the parlor and huddled urgently with Belle, Beast, and Fairy Godmother. The tension in the air was thick.

"I think we all know why we're here," said Beast, his bushy brows furrowed behind his black-framed glasses. "The people are in a panic about Hades. He almost got out."

Fairy Godmother spoke up with concern. "Who knows what he would have done if he escaped?" She *tsk*ed, imagining the horrid repercussions.

Beast, once the king himself, narrowed his eyes and stated his true feelings with authority. "We can't risk having another villain escape."

Everyone agreed, but no one had a solution.

Mal pursed her lips. "I really feel like it's my fault. I'm supposed to protect Auradon," she said. She crossed her arms against her violet wrap dress and looked down at the floor.

"You did—you do—protect Auradon," Ben said, giving Mal his full support. Mal was not to blame.

Beast shook his head, taking any thought of responsibility off Mal and placing it firmly on the impenetrable barrier—or rather on its numerous recent openings. "Every time we open the barrier, we're exposed to danger." He shuddered at the sentiment and listed the vicious villains who'd cleverly escaped the Isle. "Maleficent. Uma. Hades." This was why he'd created the Isle and its barrier in the first place: to keep their enemies out.

Beeeeeep! Ben's cell phone sounded its high-pitched alert. Ben took his phone from his blue suit pocket, checked his message, and stepped back in shock. His eyes narrowed as he reread the text. As if the day could get any worse . . .

"Maleficent's scepter and the queen's crown have been stolen," he said with dread.

Everyone else in the room gasped in unison.

"Uma," roared Beast, shaking his sizable fist in the air.

The group exchanged fearful glances at the fateful thought.

Stressed, Ben ran his hands through his sandy-brown hair. "We don't know that, Dad." But even he wasn't convinced as he said it.

Belle crossed to Beast and grabbed his arm. "When people hear this, they'll never come out of their houses!" she exclaimed, and looked out at the kingdom through the large bay window. "What do we tell them?"

The sun shone through the gauzy curtain, but the mood inside the room was dark and somber. These were troubling times. The room fell silent, and Auradon's leaders contemplated all the horrific events of the past twenty-four hours.

Belle, Beast, and Fairy Godmother looked to Mal for guidance. With utmost respect and reverence, Belle asked, "Mal, what do we do? How do we keep evil out of Auradon?" Her dread was palpable.

Mal felt the weight of everyone's eyes on her. The words she had to say were troublesome. She struggled to get them out, knowing they would change the course of Auradon forever. "I think that there's only one way to guarantee their safety. And I think that there can't be any more in and out." She hesitated, then uttered the words she never thought she'd hear herself say. "I think that we have to close the barrier forever."

Silence filled the room. But slowly, Beast, Belle, and Fairy Godmother nodded in agreement.

"No," howled Ben, refusing to accept the drastic measure.

"Son," said Beast empathetically.

"No," repeated Ben. Disheartened and discouraged, he walked to the other side of the room. His soul felt crushed. There had to be another way.

"Ben," Mal called after him.

"No, no, no, no, no," said the king. He refused to give up on the kids of the Isle.

Mal ran after Ben. "I do not want to take away your dream," she said painfully. After all, it had been her dream, too, to bring all the inculpable Isle kids to Auradon and give them a fresh start. But at what cost? "Because it was so beautiful. And it's why I fell in love with you." She looked Ben in the eye, took both of his hands in hers, and grappled with what to do. She was new to this governing thing and found it terribly difficult to work out. "But as king and queen, what's our duty?" Mal asked, already knowing the answer.

Ben's voice caught in his throat. "To protect Auradon." He shook his head with uncertainty and took Mal's hand gently in his own. This went beyond anything he'd ever expected to ask of Mal. "Do you know what this would mean? All those kids. Are you prepared for it?"

Mal's green eyes filled with tears. "I know what it means," she said, looking at Ben in defeat. How had everything gone so wrong so quickly? Hadn't it been just the day before when they were welcoming the second wave of Isle transfer students? "And no, I'm not prepared for it. I just think that we have no other choice." There was no way to open the barrier and bring Isle kids over without risking a villain breakout. So from that point forward, children of the Isle would stay condemned to the Isle. The thought brought a lump to her throat.

Beast, Belle, and Fairy Godmother listened and somberly considered the grim solution. Beast turned toward Ben. "Son, Mal's right," he said.

"I just don't think that we'd forgive ourselves if something happened," said Mal. She walked back toward the others and tugged at the dragon-and-heart pendant around her neck. She knew the true evil nature of many of the Isle's villains and imagined the worst. This was the only way she could completely protect Auradon and its people from harm.

Ben stared out the window solemnly, shook his head grimly, and with deep heartbreak let his dream of a united Auradon and Isle die.

CHAPTER EIGHT

KNOW I'M SUPPOSED TO BE GOOD AND ALL, BUT ONE HARMLESS LITTLE LIE CAN'T BE THAT BAD, RIGHT?

Evie's starter castle sat on the edge of the green forest near the outskirts of town. To no one's surprise, it was design perfection. The trendsetting decor and Isle chic vibe had already been featured in *Castle Home and Garden.* Evie's gray stone house had a terracotta-colored shingle roof, white stonework archways, blue-lattice diamond-paned windows, and a large patio lined with fruit trees where her friends loved to gather.

Evie and Mal talked in hushed tones in Evie's dreamy workroom, a breathtaking all-glass chamber with floor-to-ceiling windows and a glass roof that allowed natural light to stream in from every angle. The office had everything Evie needed to run her successful fashion design company. She stored bolts of colored fabric in a round brass caddy and kept countless spools of thread on a red wrought iron bookshelf with hand-forged scrolling. Completed tops, skirts, and frocks, waiting to be tried on, hung on a rolling rack. A framed copy of her Evie's 4 Hearts logo hung on the wall.

Evie listened with alarm as Mal confided in her, detailing all she knew about the museum break-in. Looking ever the professional in an asymmetrical polka-dot top and cropped wide-leg trousers, Evie found the news startling. "Who else knows about the scepter and the crown?" she asked.

"No one," Mal replied. "I mean, think about it. People are scared enough as it is. We have to employ these entirely new safety measures."

The news vexed Evie. She put her head in her hand. Her next question had been eating away at her since Mal had begun to tell the story. "Will this delay our bringing over more VKs?" A cloud of apprehension and concern fell over her face.

Mal avoided making eye contact. "We're talking about closing the barrier for good," she said with difficulty. She felt horrible about the words as soon as she said them. She knew Evie would be crushed.

Mal was right. Evie was appalled at the very suggestion. "But you said no." She glanced at Mal expectantly.

Mal hesitated. She'd watched Evie spend months working tirelessly on the VK Day project. Transferring kids from the Isle to Auradon meant everything to her bestie. She couldn't bear to break Evie's heart with the complicated truth. Instead, she stayed silent and lied by omission.

"I mean, the four of us are living the dream here and finally get to share it. What could be more important than that?" asked Evie.

"Yeah, I know," Mal said, raising her voice and doing her best to match Evie's outraged tone. She didn't want to appear culpable for the decision. "I mean, maybe security? Or maybe peace of mind for everyone in Auradon?" she offered tentatively. Mal hoped Evie might see things from the other perspective. But all she saw in Evie's eyes was frustration and hurt.

"Is that what they're thinking? M, are they seriously thinking that no one will ever go in or out of the Isle ever again? I mean, what, we never get to go back and see our parents?" Evie wasn't running home for mother-daughter makeovers with Evil Queen anytime soon, but she liked knowing she had the option. The idea of *never* was just so . . . well, final. "And what about these kids? We promised them they could go back and visit whenever they wanted."

"Yeah, I know," said Mal. She looked into Evie's concerned eyes and nearly crumbled under the guilt.

Evie stood up and closed the distance between them. She put her arm around Mal and searched for the positive: an Isle-born villain kid would soon sit on the throne. VKs would have a champion on the inside. Decisions about the Isle would be made by someone who'd lived on the Isle, who understood its complexities and empathized with its residents. This was a good thing—a very good thing. "M, I am so glad that you're going to be queen. You will be part of these conversations. You will stand up for the VKs. Thank you for telling me."

Evie hugged Mal, and her embrace was full of gratitude and love. "You'll be a great queen," said Evie.

Mal nodded miserably and couldn't bear to look Evie in the eye.

CHAPTER NINE

OKAY, I FEEL ABSOLUTELY HORRIBLE ABOUT LYING TO EVIE. I'VE NEVER NOT TOLD HER THE TRUTH. AT LEAST TODAY WILL BE BETTER, WITH JANE'S PARTY TO ENJOY. IT'LL BE NICE JUST TO RELAX AND CELEBRATE HER. I AM SO READY FOR NO DRAMA.

The next morning, as the warm summer sun rose over Evie's house, Evie and Jay stood in her light-strewed kitchen and packed up three straw picnic baskets for Jane's birthday party.

"Sandwich," said Evie, tossing one to Jay. He caught it one-handed, like the skilled athlete he was. His short-sleeved maroon hoodie showed off his biceps in action.

Evie, who'd chosen to wear a sporty shorts romper to the summer soiree, laughed, then started to playfully pluck apples from the fruit basket and toss them to Jay with perfect precision. He looked up as Carlos, all smiles and cheerfulness, walked into the kitchen.

"Good morning," Carlos said with a spring in his step. Wearing a black-and-white diagonally striped shirt and white jeans, Carlos had clearly put effort into looking extra handsome for the party. Carlos wanted Jane's day to be as wonderful as she was. Jane was always doing thoughtful things to make everyone else feel special, and that day he planned to do the same for her. He'd picked a bouquet of wild bluebells that matched the color of her eyes, bought several giant birthday balloons as cheery as her smile, and ordered a yellow layer cake with vanilla buttercream, light blue frosting, and pink fondant bows—her favorite.

"I really think she's gonna like the cake, you guys," said Carlos, who'd had *Happy Bibbidi-Bobbidi Birthday, Jane!* scrolled in icing along the top.

"Oh, yeah?" asked Evie.

Carlos had a huge grin on his face as he walked to the pink bakery box, but suddenly, he frowned with surprise. A giant slice of the cake was missing. "Oh, no! Who got into Jane's cake?" he asked, exasperated.

What kind of evil person would eat someone else's birthday cake?

Celia and Dizzy sat beneath the lilac vines on Evie's back patio and laughed with delight. Their hands and faces were covered in telltale icing, and cake crumbs cascaded down their bright party dresses. "Dee-licious," Dizzy said, giggling.

"I especially liked the lack of dirt," chirped Celia, who had once received an actual mud pie on her birthday.

"And the lack of flies," Dizzy agreed, licking her fingers. Sprinkles tasted way better than bugs.

Celia took another huge bite and nodded in agreement. "Want some?" She offered her plate to Dizzy, who had already finished every last crumb of cake on her own plate.

"Thank you," Dizzy said, and happily gobbled up more. The two daughters of villains agreed: cake was definitely the best thing about life in Auradon so far.

Mouthwatering birthday cake was no longer a novelty for Mal, but she was looking forward to Jane's party for other reasons. The past couple of days had been über-intense, and she gladly welcomed a few hours with her friends at the Enchanted Lake. She'd wrapped Jane's present in a big purple gift bag and was wearing new purple denim skorts for the special occasion. But no sooner had Mal exited the glass French doors to Evie's place than she was greeted by a mysterious explosion of billowing pink smoke.

"I was hoping you were home." Mal heard the familiar voice of Sleeping Beauty's daughter, whipped her head around, and stared at Audrey incredulously. Audrey looked utterly villainous. She cradled Maleficent's scepter in her right hand and, with an air of entitlement, wore the queen's majestic sapphire crown on top of her magenta ombre hair.

"Huh? Is this a joke?" asked Mal, sincerely wondering if the precious princess was off to another one of her lame costume balls. "What are you doing with the crown and the scepter?"

Audrey glared at Mal, spite radiating from her eyes, and extinguished any ideas of humor. "Well, I wanted them, so I took them. You of all people should understand that, Mal," she hissed, taking a thinly veiled jab at Mal for stealing Ben from her.

Mal looked Audrey up and down suspiciously. The orb of Maleficent's scepter glowed venomously, and Audrey seemed to be drinking in its power. Mal tried not to freak out, but this was bad—really, really bad. Mal was all too familiar with the destructive powers of her mother's loathsome staff.

Audrey glared at her nemesis. Then she crouched down, cradling the scepter, as if to cast a spell.

"Wait. Audrey, stop. Don't use that!" Mal begged, desperately trying to think of a way to disarm her.

"I thought you liked spells," purred Audrey, relishing her upper hand.

Mal's alarm heightened. She had to convince Audrey to relinquish the scepter before the vengeful princess did something she'd regret. Perhaps she should appeal to her as a friend. Mal tried to employ her sweetest-sounding voice. "Okay, Audrey—"

Audrey interrupted Mal right there. She wasn't buying Mal's chummy act, not for a minute. "Quiet," she ordered. With a savage blow, she struck the glowing scepter on the ground and released a worrying shower of bright sparks.

Mal genuinely quivered. "That's not a toy!" she exclaimed. "It's dangerous."

Audrey's eyes teemed with evil intent. "I *want* to be dangerous. My life was perfect until you stole it! And then Auradon turned its back on me." Audrey pivoted in place, whipped around her luscious hair, and stormed away with attitude. "It's time for a little payback," she muttered ominously.

"Audrey, wait," shouted Mal. Desperation filled her voice.

Audrey spun around, threw back her head, and cackled. She waved the luminous scepter in Mal's direction, then cursed her with a flash of light. When the pink smoke cleared, its effect left Mal speechless. The hex had transformed Mal into a shriveled old woman. Mal's glossy purple hair had turned a sickly shade of gray, and her once-porcelain skin was covered with deep wrinkles and liver spots. Her chic purple vest was replaced with a ratty wool cloak. Mal looked down at her withered hands and winced.

Audrey soaked up Mal's pained reaction and laughed with glee. "Think Ben will love you now, you old hag?" Audrey lifted the scepter to the sky triumphantly. "You'll pay the price for what you did, and so will all of Auradon."

Alerted by the commotion, Evie, Jay, Carlos, and Celia burst out of the house. They stopped short on the driveway when they saw Audrey in possession of the magical objects, then gawked when they saw Mal's monstrous makeover.

Audrey took a moment to bask in everyone's shock, then snickered, twirled around, and disappeared in a puffy cloud of pink smoke. "So long, suckers." Revenge really was glorious.

Jay rushed to Mal's aid but accidentally recoiled in revulsion when he saw her up close. "Whoa! Ah, you might want to think of a spell for that." He winced.

"There's no spell that can reverse the curse of the scepter," responded Mal. Her voice sounded gravelly and old.

"Well, that's a shame," Carlos muttered, and looked away with a grimace.

Mal shook her head of wiry gray hair, then squinted her eyes, crow's-feet and all, toward the remaining wisps of Audrey's pink smoke. "Forget about me. Audrey's out for revenge. Auradon's in danger." Mal knew from firsthand experience with her mother: that scepter was dangerous in the hands of a woman scorned.

"What should we do?" asked Evie.

Mal looked at her frantic friends. "The only thing more powerful than the scepter is Hades's ember."

"Like he's just going to hand it over to you after you blew him back to the Isle," Jay said, raising one eyebrow.

"No one knows where his lair is," said Evie as she crossed her arms over her chest.

Celia piped up. "I do. I'm his errand rat. I've got the key at my dad's."

Mal pointed at Celia with authority—well, as much authority as an old hunchback could muster. "You're coming."

"But I just got here," Celia said disappointedly. She had expected to revel in more of Auradon's beauty and riches before returning to the Isle. And also to eat more cake.

In truth, returning to the Isle wasn't anyone's first choice for how to spend the day, but there was no other way. They had to retrieve the ember to safeguard Auradon.

Just then, Dizzy appeared in the doorway, holding Squeaky's and Squirmy's hands. They were all spruced up and ready to leave for Jane's party. "Mal?" asked Dizzy, her voice cracking with confusion.

As realization hit, Dizzy shrieked in terror. The twins buried their faces in fear.

Evie's heart went out to the terrified kids. "Dizzy, stay here and take care of the twins. We'll be right back and everything is going to be just fine. Go inside," she instructed, hoping the younger VKs bought her fake-confidence act. Then she turned to Carlos, Jay, and Celia. "Guys, go get your stuff."

While the others ran inside Evie's castle, Mal turned and whispered to Evie, "Really, how bad is it?" She flashed a near-toothless grin.

"You age beautifully," Evie reassured her with a quick smile. "Now let's just get you into something fabulous, okay?" Evie was halfway to the front door when she realized elderly Mal walked at an extremely slow pace. She took a few steps back to help her friend.

Mal had always known she and Evie would be best friends until a ripe old age. She just hadn't planned on that old age coming so soon.

A little while later, senior citizen Mal, Evie, Jay, and Carlos peeled through the forest on their custom-detailed motorbikes, with Celia riding on the back of Mal's. On a normal day, the VKs loved to take their tricked-out bikes for a spin, but there was no joy in that day's ride as they headed toward their unfortunate mission. The group, all wearing helmets in their signature colors, pulled to a stop on a rocky bluff and looked out across Auradon Bay. Not one of them was excited to return home.

Mal lifted her safety goggles. Her wrinkled eyes flashed green and she incanted from memory: *"Noble steeds, proud and fair, you shall take us anywhere."* With a zing of enchantment, the motorbikes roared to life and magically zipped across the surface of the sea toward the Isle. Celia had not seen that coming in her fortune cards.

Moments later, Carlos's dog, Dude, scurried onto the bluff and saw his master's bike floating toward the horizon. "Carloooooooos!" the talking dog howled forlornly. "You're gonna miss Jane's birthday!" But he was too late.

CHAPTER TEN

A ND A VERY UNHAPPY BIRTHDAY TO
POOR JANE...

It was the perfect day for a birthday party at the
Enchanted Lake, and Jane's guests were having a
blast. They splashed in the crystalline green water
and enjoyed cupcakes off a three-tiered pastry stand.
Several girls in summer dresses gathered around a
crystal punch bowl. A periwinkle banner reading
HAPPY BIRTHDAY, JANE hung above their heads. The
banner, of course, was decorated with pink bows.
Jane matched the decorations, wearing a new off-
the-shoulder pinstriped romper with a fuchsia bow
at the waist. The party was a rollicking success, but
the birthday girl looked a touch sad. All her birthday
wishes hadn't exactly come true.

"Looks like Carlos forgot about your birthday," said Chad. The daft prince leaned over the lake and filled a giant squirt gun with water, preparing to surprise his next victim.

Jane had been almost 100 percent sure Carlos would be there. "Well, maybe not. Maybe he just took the wrong trail or something. Or you know what? They probably don't celebrate birthdays on the Isle. Maybe it's like a cultural thing," Jane reasoned.

Chad snickered. "Yeah, or maybe he just forgot your birthday. You never know."

Jane wasn't enjoying their little chat. "Hey, Chad, look. There's people taking selfies," she pointed out in an effort to distract him.

"Selfies, guys! Wait, wait, wait, wait, wait. Wait for me!" Chad yelped. He couldn't stand the thought of missing out on a good photo op. He handed his precious squirt gun to Jane and sprinted up the hill to join the other students. Jane smiled to herself, pleased to be rid of him. Now if only Carlos, Mal, and the others would arrive, her birthday would be perfect.

Without warning, a fierce wind swept through the

party with a whoosh. The music died instantly, and up on the grass, a cloud of threatening pink smoke swirled. Jane's guests gasped as Audrey appeared, wearing the queen's crown and holding Maleficent's scepter.

"Anyone save me guacamole?" she asked a surprised young man. "No? Someone forgot to invite me." Audrey swanned around Jane's party just like Maleficent had at the christening years earlier. She plucked a blue-frosted cupcake out of a party guest's hands and chucked it to the ground with spite.

Jane frowned. Audrey was not the surprise guest she was hoping to see.

Audrey smirked. "Don't expect Mal," she told the birthday girl. "She's not feeling herself." Jane furrowed her brow with worry. "Does that make you sad? Ruin everything?" Audrey asked with an insolent tone.

Audrey made a show of spinning the scepter and pointing it at the detestable party guests. "Mindless little drones. How could you forget what she did to us? How could you forget that I was supposed to be your queen?" she bellowed.

Audrey raised the staff and was about to release havoc on the party when Chad scampered down the hill, waving his hands in the air, frantic to catch her attention. He darted to Audrey's side. "Time out, time out. First off, great new look. I absolutely love the feathers," he said, and winked at Audrey.

Audrey glared at him with contempt. Chad kept rambling.

"Before you do whatever you're going to do, I was wondering if maybe you wanted a loyal boyfriend by your side?" he asked.

Audrey rolled her eyes.

"Partner in crime? Sidekick?" Chad abandoned all hope of seeming like a brave and gallant prince and pleaded with Audrey. "Or maybe just a lackey to do your bidding. Change tires? Or smoothie runs?" Chad gave Audrey his best puppy dog eyes, the ones she had never been able to resist when they'd dated.

"You can be useful. Fine. Stand behind me," Audrey conceded. Chad scampered behind Audrey as she gazed over the rest of the loathsome party. "If Auradon likes to forget so much, you'll love this!"

Audrey strolled menacingly between the scattered

guests and sang a creepy rendition of "Happy Birthday." Her voice was thick with vengeance. Each time she stopped and stared at a group of teenagers, ominous fog rolled in and put the cluster of students to sleep on the spot. Haughty and imperious, Audrey paraded around the lakeside and spread her curse of endless sleep across the entire party. The spell gave new meaning to the phrase *slumber party*. Once all the guests were asleep, Audrey stood on top of a rocky cliff and stared down at Jane, who stood alone in the pavilion. *"Happy birthday, dear Jane. Happy birthday to you."*

The magical fog rolled closer and closer to the birthday girl. It was sure to put her to sleep the moment it touched her. But Jane, ever so clever, was one step ahead of the sorceresses. *The Enchanted Lake!* she thought, and waded into the sparkling magical water.

"Audrey?" asked Chad.

"Sweet dreams," Audrey incanted, savoring the success of her evil plan.

But Audrey didn't see Jane's escape into the lake. The birthday girl held her breath underwater for what felt like forever. Finally, she exhaled and rose to the surface. Gasping for air, she watched Audrey slam her scepter ruthlessly into the ground and disappear with Chad in a cloud of smoke.

It was official, Jane thought. This was the worst birthday party ever.

King Ben stood in his palace bedroom. He was already late for Jane's party. His meeting had taken more time than he'd hoped. But now he was finished with his official duties for the day, had traded in his formal suit for a casual navy-and-yellow striped rugby shirt, and could finally go have some fun with his friends. He retrieved Jane's present from his shelf and looked around to see if he was forgetting anything.

Ben's cell phone rang. "Hey, Jane, I'm on my way to the party," he said apologetically. "The meetings ran long."

Jane paced along the lake's stone platform and held her pink phone to her ear. She wished her biggest problem was tardy party guests. "No, no. Stay where you are, Ben. Audrey's got the scepter. And everyone's asleep," she blurted frantically. She was still trying to understand how the good girl had turned so evil so quickly. "I'm gonna call Mom and tell her to get the wand." She hung up quickly and, in a frenzy, began to dial Fairy Godmother.

"Is Mal with you? Jane? Jane?" Ben asked an empty phone line. A panicked expression fell over his face.

CHAPTER ELEVEN

Dr. F's arcade is seriously the best . . . and for Celia, it's home.

The VKs' four motorbikes landed amid the lively atmosphere of the French Quarter. Mal removed her bike helmet and immediately brought her hands to her face. The deep wrinkles, saggy skin, and old-lady hair had been replaced by her flawless complexion and signature lush purple locks. The powerful curse of Audrey's scepter had been broken. "Heeeeeeey, I'm me again!" she said with a grateful laugh.

"Duh, evil magic doesn't work here. Kinda the point," said Celia.

"Woo, welcome back," Evie said. She threw her arm around her pal, relieved that the spell had lifted.

"Thank you," said Mal, ecstatic to be back to her

old self. She smiled, then followed Celia as she led them down a dark run-down lane.

Celia looked around her hood and realized it felt good to be home. She walked past her fortune-teller table and stopped suddenly in front of a magenta-and-gray-painted door with PA DERANJE stamped across it. For those new to the French Quarter, that meant *Do Not Disturb*. Celia was all smiles as she knocked six times in a rhythmic pattern. *Tap-pi-ty tap tap tap.* It was answered by a second series of elaborate knocks. *Tap tap tap tap tap.* The whole thing was very cool and cryptic; the veteran VKs were impressed. Celia knocked out one more secret code and the thick steel door slid open. The five travelers pushed through a set of opaque curtains, then entered the shrouded hideaway through the open mouth of a forty-foot-tall laughing carnival mask. DR. FACILIER'S VOODOO ARCADE was spelled out above them in neon lights. Several of the letters had burned out, but that only added to the atmosphere. The rowdy room was packed with villain kids of all ages. There was no arguing that Dr. Facilier's business was booming.

Dr. Facilier, looking rakish in a magenta crushed-velvet suit and a silk top hat with a purple plume, greeted his daughter with pure delight. "Hey," he said, tossing his walking stick to a nearby customer. He rushed to meet Celia on the arcade floor, where the two busted into an impressive coordinated dance. The adorably elaborate routine was clearly the way the pair greeted each other all the time. With the secret salutation complete, Dr. Facilier hugged his daughter tightly. "Come here, you little rascal." His face was illuminated with the kind of joy brought on by an excellent surprise. It was clear from Celia's giant grin that she was equally elated to see her pops.

Mal and her friends took in the sweet family scene and exchanged heartfelt glances. Dr. F and Celia were like two thieves in a pod. It was so different from the other VKs' experience with their own parents. They weren't used to seeing love like this in a villain family. It really was quite something.

Dr. Facilier glanced slyly at his celebrity guests, leaned into his daughter, and whispered, "What kind of hustle you got going with the shiny people?" His eyes glinted with mischievous approval.

"No hustle," Celia said, smiling. "I got friends on the other side."

"I hear you," said her dad, his eyebrows dancing with understanding.

Celia scanned the room. She looked past mysterious pin dolls, half-melted candles, vintage strands of beads, and assorted glass trinkets and finally focused on a wall near her fortune-telling nook. She headed straight for it, the tassels and pom-poms that adorned her outfit swaying as she walked. She retrieved a mysterious skull-shaped key from the wall and placed it around her neck.

Dr. Facilier looked at her questioningly.

"We're on a mission," she explained conspiratorially. "I'm kind of a major player. So that's why I can't stay long," she bragged brashly, hoping to impress her father.

It worked. Dr. Facilier looked at his mischievous daughter with what was clearly pride. "Just make sure you get your cut," he said, beaming.

Toward the front of the arcade, Carlos stood in

ON VK DAY, MAL, EVIE, CARLOS, AND JAY RETURNED TO THE ISLE OF THE LOST TO ENCOURAGE ALL VILLAIN KIDS TO APPLY FOR ONE OF THE FOUR COVETED SPOTS AT AURADON PREP.

DIZZY WAS THRILLED TO BE OFFICIALLY ACCEPTED TO AURADON PREP.

MAL SCANNED THE HORIZON FOR SIGNS OF UMA'S RETURN.

AFTER HADES ALMOST ESCAPED FROM THE ISLE WHILE THE BARRIER WAS DOWN, AURADON'S LEADERS GATHERED TO DISCUSS HOW TO KEEP THE KINGDOM SAFE FROM EVIL.

HEARTBROKEN BY BEN'S ENGAGEMENT, AUDREY DECIDED SHE'D FIND A WAY TO WEAR THE QUEEN'S CROWN.

LURED BY THE EVIL POWER OF MALEFICENT'S SCEPTER, AUDREY TRANSFORMED INTO A WICKED VILLAINESS.

DIZZY, SQUEAKY, AND SQUIRMY WERE HORRIFIED WHEN THEY SAW THE RESULTS OF AUDREY'S FIRST SPELL.

CELIA LED MAL TO HADES'S LAIR IN AN OLD MINE SHAFT ON THE ISLE OF THE LOST.

TO STOP AUDREY'S EVIL REIGN, MAL TRIED TO STEAL HADES'S EMBER, THE ONLY MAGICAL OBJECT POWERFUL ENOUGH TO DEFEAT MALEFICENT'S SCEPTER.

DURING A SCUFFLE, HADES'S EMBER SLIPPED FROM MAL'S HAND INTO THE SEA, ONLY TO BE RETRIEVED BY UMA.

THE VKS RETURNED TO AURADON TO FIND EVERYONE UNDER
AUDREY'S SLEEPING SPELL.

TOGETHER, THE VKS AND PIRATES FOUGHT AN EPIC BATTLE AGAINST
AN ARMY OF ARMORED SUITS THAT HAD COME TO LIFE, COURTESY OF
ONE OF AUDREY'S INCANTATIONS.

THE VKS ARRIVED AT FAIRY COTTAGE TOO LATE TO APPREHEND AUDREY.

WITH ALL THE COMMOTION, CARLOS ALMOST MISSED JANE'S BIRTHDAY, BUT HE MADE IT UP TO HER WITH A SPECIAL GIFT.

ONCE EVERYONE WAS REUNITED, THEY PUT A PLAN IN PLACE TO END AUDREY'S REIGN.

UMA AND HARRY WATCHED AS MAL TRANSFORMED INTO A DRAGON TO SAVE AURADON.

front of an ancient antenna television and put in the two tokens it required to start. The beat-up set sprang to life and an Auradon newscast revealed that evil things were afoot across the sea. "Alerts of a sleeping spell keep coming in as it spreads throughout Auradon," said the anchor, reporting live from the circular driveway at Auradon Prep.

"Uh, guys, come look at this," said Carlos. Dread filled his face.

Mal, Evie, Jay, and Carlos gathered around and watched the news in dismay. "There are rumors that Sleeping Beauty's daughter, Audrey, is behind the spell," continued the reporter. "We are trying to discover who is responsible for these vicious lies and which evil villain perpetrated this evil."

The anchorman cocked his head, listened to his earphone, and spoke with urgency. "We have an update. It's moving this way! It's moving . . ."

Mal, Evie, Jay, and Carlos sprinted outside, ready to rush back to Auradon and save the kingdom. There was just one problem: they had no way to get there.

Harry Hook, Gil, and two of their nasty pirate buds sat astride the VKs' motorbikes. Based on the laws of the street, their bikes were pirate booty now. The scallywags had even stolen their helmets.

"Wow. Rookie mistake," said Carlos, feeling foolish. The VKs knew better than to leave anything of value sitting out in the open around the Isle.

Captain Hook's son, who had a permanent smarmy smirk etched across his face, raised his left arm and mock-saluted Jay with his fake hook. "Long time no see," said Harry, his words drowning in his Isle pirate accent.

"Get off my bike, Hook," Jay said. As the pirate rode off, Jay leapt deftly over random street rubbish to run after his bike.

"Catch me if you can, Jay," Harry dared him. His striking green eyes sparkled as he scooted down the French Quarter avenue.

Gil, son of Gaston, drove off next, wearing a brown leather shirt over his sizable biceps and a brown bandana over his matted dirty-blond hair. He took his hands off the handlebars and waved his muscular arms in the air as he drove by.

Jay surveyed the French Quarter street, formulated a plan, and then, as if calling a play on the tourney field, instructed the others where to go. "Over the roofs, we'll cut them off!" he exclaimed, and scurried up the side of an old shack. Evie and Carlos followed Jay's lead. Celia started to join the fray, but Mal grabbed the collar of the little fortune-teller's splashy jacket and brought her to a swift halt. "Hey, hey, hey," Mal said. "They got this. You and me gotta go find the ember."

"Good timing." Celia snapped her fingers. "It's right about his naptime." She turned on the wedge heel of her magenta bootie and led Mal in the opposite direction, through the maze of twisted alleys.

CHAPTER TWELVE

BARKING GUARD DOGS AND DESCENDING INTO A MINE SHAFT AREN'T EXACTLY MY IDEA OF A GOOD TIME....

Mal and Celia stood at the locked entrance of a run-down old mine shaft. It reeked of *bad idea*. The wire fence was marked with the same unnerving skull graphic as was on the pin Hades wore to fasten his chiton. Mal recoiled at the sight. Her eyes focused on the ominous NO TRESPASSING and GET LOST signs that covered the gate. She paused at one that read BEWARE OF DOG with a crude drawing of a foreboding Cerberus. "Hey, how big is that dog?" she asked.

"You'll see." Celia placed the skull-shaped key in the rusted lock and slowly opened the corroded gate. It squeaked. She entered the dark, dank shaft and motioned for Mal to follow.

Mal looked down the dodgy passageway with concern. She feared what lay at the other end of the shaft.

Celia did nothing to calm those fears. "Stay quiet," the young girl warned ominously. "It echoes like crazy in here."

The dog's barking interrupted the silence, causing Mal to jump. She had a terrible feeling about this.

"Come on," Celia said, beckoning.

Celia grabbed a dirt-covered mining helmet, flicked on the headlamp, and climbed onto the front seat of a rusted-out rail cycle. It resembled a tandem bicycle that had been affixed to the base of an old mine car. Mal breathed deeply, grabbed a mining hat, and hopped onto the back seat. The things she was willing to do for Auradon . . .

Celia checked the jalopy's jerry-rigged lanterns and released the brake, and the girls pedaled into the craggy tunnel, which grew smaller with every inch they descended. When the shaft became too narrow for the mine cycle, they hopped off the rig, removed their mining helmets, and tiptoed toward a small tunnel opening. The insistent dog barking kept Mal on edge. Celia disappeared down the chute. Mal hesitated for a moment, then followed close behind. The girls paused at the mouth of the tunnel and surveyed Hades's ramshackle chamber, which lay below. Mal was not impressed.

The god of the Underworld had converted an abandoned mining cave into his sooty make-do personal lair. The rocky walls were slick with minerals. Rotting support timbers stood throughout. An azure scarf covered a wobbly lampshade, bathing the entire room in a blue haze. With black sunglasses covering his blue eyes, Hades sat deep asleep on a shoddy throne. The immortal god's feet were perched on the armrest.

The vicious dog bark continued to pierce the air. Mal leapt with alarm and looked around frantically for the rabid Cerberus—until she noticed Celia indicating an old record that was circling on a dusty turntable. Okay, so she didn't need to beware of an actual dog. Still, Mal couldn't help feeling that the mission was ill-fated.

Celia locked eyes with Mal, nodded to the side, then pointed. Mal followed her gaze. Smack-dab behind Hades's snoring head sat a small etched dish that held the coveted blue ember. Mal looked at Celia and nodded confirmation. Then she slid into the villain's private quarters.

Mal crept nimbly through the disheveled chamber and angled toward the blue ember. The space was dead quiet except for the canine recording, which rasped and scratched in an irksome way. Annoyed by the grating sound, Celia decided to lift the needle on the prehistoric record player—just as Mal stepped behind the slumbering Hades. The needle scratched with an *eeeeee!*

Hades awoke with a start at the sound. He lifted his sunglasses; his blue eyes shone clear and alert. "What are you doing here?" he bellowed.

His voice sent chills down Mal's spine. Caught, she froze in place and desperately searched her brain for a clever excuse. Then Mal noticed Hades wasn't speaking to her.

"I noticed you were low on canned corn," said Celia. It was a plausible pretext for Hades's errand girl. Unruffled, Celia walked right up to Hades, reached into her coat, and confidently tossed an expired can of corn at the once-powerful villain. Mal had to hand it to Celia; that girl was one fearless, smooth criminal.

With Hades's attention directed at Celia, Mal seized her opportunity to take the ember. After everything Mal had done in Auradon to prove her goodness, it felt funny to be stealing again. But she reasoned that this small crime was okay because it was for a good cause. Drawing on all her old thieving skills, Mal squatted down, stretched out her arm, and, without making a peep, nabbed Hades's ember from its battered and tarnished silver stand.

Unfortunately, her action didn't go unnoticed. As if he had eyes in the back of his spiked blue hair, Hades raised his hand and grabbed Mal's wrist behind him. He sneered forebodingly and snatched the ember right out of her hand. Rats, he was good!

Mal, caught in Hades's vise grip, had no choice. The moment she'd been dreading more than any other had finally arrived. Her stomach dropped. There was nothing left to do but face it head-on.

"Hello, Dad." The words felt foreign on Mal's tongue. While it took a lot to shock Celia, her mouth dropped open in disbelief.

The name sounded strange to Hades's ears as well. He let the word roll around in his head for a moment before responding. If it affected him, he didn't let it show. He simply removed his sunglasses and waved nonchalantly at his daughter. His nails were painted blue.

"Quite a show you put on the other day," said Hades, sizing up his daughter. He bored into Mal's soul with his eyes.

"Back atcha," Mal said flippantly to her estranged father. Mal might have been trembling inside, but she refused to show her father an ounce of fear. He didn't deserve that kind of satisfaction. She hadn't seen Hades in years, and this was twice in one week. Lucky her.

"I was just coming to see you," Hades said, flashing his magnetic smile. He could be so charismatic when he wanted to be.

"Really? Wonder why. Is it because I'm going to be queen?" Mal said. Her tone brimmed with contempt.

Hades shook off his daughter's implication. "Now, Mal, don't be bitter."

"You abandoned me when I was a baby," she said,

crossing her arms over her chest. She had every right to be bitter.

"No, no," Hades said, sounding ornery. "I left your mother. She's not the easiest person to get along with."

"Ya think?" spat Mal.

"Ya see?" said Hades. "We have something in common already. We both hate your mother." He laughed at his own warped sense of father-daughter bonding.

"No, I don't hate my mother," said Mal, her eyes challenging Hades. "She may be an evil lunatic, but at least she stuck around." Mal surprised even herself by defending her mom. She didn't usually land on Team Maleficent. But this was different. This wasn't about Maleficent; it was about Hades and the indisputable fact that he had never been there for her. She looked at her father with disdain.

Hades's veins bulged from his neck and he erupted in aggression. "Oh, boo-hoo, wake up and smell the stink. You think you've had it rough?" he said, recalling his glory days. "I used to be a god. I had an entire world which bore my name. And now I have nothing." For emphasis, he threw to the ground the can of corn, which landed with a clank. "You have no idea what that feels like."

Mal held her own in the fight. "Really? Because for sixteen years I had nothing. And now I have a whole world. But unless I get that ember, it's game over." She stuck out her hand expectantly.

Hades was unimpressed with Mal's trivial teenage drama. As a god, he'd seen everything over the centuries. A destroyed kingdom and a lost boyfriend—those were ho-hum problems. He wasn't about to pity his daughter or show her kindness. He'd parent her the way he always had. "I gave you everything by giving you nothing," he claimed with a surly sneer. By his logic, his absence all those years had only made Mal stronger. His daughter was a problem-solver now because he hadn't been there to run and fix things for her. Or at least that was what he told himself.

Mal fumed. Did Hades expect her to believe that feeble explanation? Come on. Hades had done whatever was best for him, and they both knew it. The only reason she was paying him a visit was that she needed something—and that something wasn't him. It was his ember—to save her friends.

For all their differences, when they stood in such proximity, both brutally speaking their minds, the father-daughter resemblance was uncanny. Hades noticed it and reached for Mal, but she pulled away.

"Do you want to make up for being a lousy dad? Give me the ember," Mal said.

"The ember only works for me," snapped Hades.

"No. It'll work. We're blood," said Mal, suddenly remembering and feeling very grateful for her Auradon Prep class the Study of Magical Objects.

Hades held up the ember, rolled it between his fingers, and taunted his daughter. "You're only half Hades. The ember won't do everything for you that it does for me."

Mal looked her father straight in the eyes. "I'll take my chances," she countered, calling his bluff.

Hades stared at Mal for a good while and in that moment understood that this was his chance to do something fatherly. He whirled the ember around his fingers, handed it to his daughter, and warned her, "If it gets wet, it's game over."

Mal snatched the ember and motioned to Celia, and the two girls were out of there.

Hades stared at the tunnel entrance for a moment and allowed the smallest flash of pride to cross his face. "That's my girl," he mumbled to himself.

Celia and Mal walked through the dark tunnel. "I guess that's the reason why he's always asking about you," said Celia.

Mal stopped in her tracks and raised her eyebrows, surprised to learn Hades had ever shown an interest in her. "Evie is the only one who knows that he's my dad," she told Celia. "And as far as I'm concerned, he doesn't even exist." Yet here she was, clutching his ember tightly in her hand.

Mal followed Celia through the mine, lost in thought.

CHAPTER THIRTEEN

I GUESS IT STANDS TO REASON THAT IF MY FRIENDS AND I COULD CHOOSE GOOD, THAT GOODY-GOODY CLASS PRESIDENT COULD CHOOSE EVIL.

Ben held his cell phone in his right hand, ran his left hand through his hair, and paced his palace bedroom. He was in full king mode, all authority and confidence, calling the shots and getting things done. "No, no. I want the Auradon guard handing out gas masks. . . . Well, not everyone is asleep." He threw down his phone and pointed at the royal attendant who stood watch at the entranceway. "Find out if anyone's seen Audrey."

The young man nodded in acknowledgement and headed toward the door.

Suffocating from frustration, the king unsnapped

the collar of his blue-and-yellow leather jacket and fell into his chair with an agitated sigh. "And find out if she has a list of demands," Ben ordered.

Ben heard her voice before he saw her. "Just one, Benny Boo. I demand my life back," Audrey said.

Ben spun around, startled. Audrey creeped behind him. Her wicked transformation was utterly shocking. She looked stunningly evil.

"I have a proposition. I'll wake everybody up right now—under one itty-bitty condition, Benny Boo," she said, her eyes glinting with a dark scheme. Her fingers crawled up Ben's arm until she held his face in her hand. "Make me your queen and we'll rule side by side." From Audrey's perspective, she belonged on that throne; it was her rightful place in history. She, not Mal, was born and bred for the royal life.

Ben looked at Audrey like she was off-kilter. He slowly removed her hand from his cheek. "Did someone put a spell on you?" he asked his former girlfriend. "Just tell me who and I'll—"

"What? Marry them?" Audrey quipped, and giggled at her own joke. "Most people get dumped because they're not good enough. I wasn't *bad* enough. How do you like me now, Benny Boo?" She twirled around and modeled her ravishing new style for her ex. Gone were Audrey's signature pink frills; they had been replaced by deep mauve, black lace, and black feathers. She looked even more the part of the alluring enchantress than she had at the museum, with the queen's crown glinting on her head.

Ben shrugged earnestly. He didn't care for her metamorphosis. "I liked the old Audrey better," he said honestly. "She wouldn't want to hurt Auradon. Just give me the scepter and I'll forgive you." He meant it. Ben's sole goal was to keep his kingdom secure. He was willing to pardon Audrey in exchange for the guaranteed safety of his citizens. King Ben held out his open hand and hoped Audrey would come to her senses.

Audrey grew furious. "You'll forgive me?" She pointed her finger at him. "I don't think so! Sleeping is too good for you!"

Her eyes gleamed with malicious intent. A snarl took over her face. She thrust her scepter toward Ben and released a crackling hex. She grinned at the results with glee. That spell had worked better than she'd expected.

Next she turned her sights on Auradon City. Audrey stood on Ben's balcony, peered out over the entire kingdom with mad delight, and released a condemning curse on all the people below. "Sleeping is too good for Auradon." A menacing flash blanketed the kingdom.

At that very moment, Fairy Godmother was running up the steps of the museum to obtain her wand. As the evil magic washed over her, the Auradon Prep headmistress was turned instantly to stone. The same frozen fate befell hundreds of others all around the kingdom. Audrey was quite pleased with her sorcery.

CHAPTER FOURTEEN

I KNEW THAT SHRIMPY GIRL WOULD BE BACK, UGH!

Mal and Celia returned to the Isle's destitute Bridge Plaza to meet up with Jay, Carlos, and Evie.

"All right, let's get in, let's get out," said Mal. They needed to open the barrier and sneak through without any trouble.

Jay clicked the remote, the barrier flickered open, and they darted through with stealthy moves.

Mal squeezed Hades's ember tightly in her palm as she crossed onto the bridge to Auradon, desperate for the ember to work for her as it had for Hades. And it did. The ember ignited into dancing blue flames the moment it hit the magical land. Then, with a flash, the glowing power shot straight through Mal. Its effect on her was instantaneous. Her signature purple hair became streaked with blue tones, and her purple vest turned midnight blue. Even her wedge high-tops and fingerless gloves boasted painted blue flames. Mal looked down, stared at her altered clothes in shock, then twirled a strand of her bluish hair with intense fascination. "Huh," she said. She guessed there was more of her dad in her than she'd realized.

Evie, Carlos, Jay, and Celia circled Mal, checking out her new look from every angle.

"Wow," Evie said, impressed.

"Man, that thing packs a punch," said Carlos, nodding toward the glowing ember.

Before any of them could question why Hades's ember had affected Mal as it had, Jay gasped, then turned the group's attention to the Isle side of the bridge. "Look," he shouted with urgency.

Mal was grateful for the distraction until she saw what Jay had spotted.

Harry Hook and his sidekick, Gil, somersaulted through the closing Isle barrier and landed safely on the bridge. It was just as Beast had predicted: every time they opened the barrier, another villain—or, in this case, villains—escaped.

"We made it!" exclaimed Gil, his eyes wide with amazement. For the first time in his life, he'd stepped foot off the Isle.

"Bro!" yapped Harry as he and Gil bro-hugged it out. They'd done it! They'd busted out of the Isle. Harry turned toward Mal and her friends. "Hey, guys," Harry said, chuckling. "We just came for a wee visit."

Carlos and Jay tried to block the pirates' path. As the two groups collided mid-bridge, Celia hung back coolly and enjoyed watching the fracas like a spectator. According to her father, there was no sense in picking sides until a clear winner was declared.

Mal, on the other hand, tried to intervene. "No, no, no, no, no," she uttered, hoping to keep the pirates from going any farther. Harry shoved Carlos in an effort to get by. His strong push sent Carlos tumbling into Mal. Mal staggered off-balance, causing the ember to jostle free from her grip. She desperately tried to grab the escaping ember, but Harry's hook scooped around her fumbling hand before she could nab it. The bright blue ember sailed high into the air and out of Mal's reach.

"Noooooooooo," screamed Mal. She watched helplessly as it plummeted toward the deep dark water below. Any chance of saving Auradon from Audrey was extinguished the moment the ember got wet. Mal waited with agony for the telltale splash.

But the dreaded splash never came. Instead, a long, slimy turquoise tentacle emerged from the sea. It stretched to its impressive full length and skillfully snatched the ember out of the air. With a whoosh, Uma, in her part-octopus form, rose grandly from the rough waters and gripped the powerful ember.

Mal had to hand it to the sea witch: she knew how to make a splashy entrance.

Uma looked magnificent, wilder, and more in her element than she had at Cotillion. She wore a turquoise sweetheart-necked bodice that perfectly framed her mother's golden shell necklace. Her tentacles swirled through the water with grace and ease. She tossed back her long turquoise hair, which was braided at the crown of her head and fell loose below her waist.

"Drop something?" she asked with a wry smile. The ember sizzled, dulled, and grew weaker in her dripping grasp.

Mal was unsure if she should feel relieved or panicked to see Hades's ember in Uma's hand—er, tentacle. For all the ways she had imagined Uma's returning to Auradon, she'd never dreamt up this scenario—her archnemesis cradling the single object that could save the kingdom. This definitely called for panic.

"It can't get wet. Give it back before it goes out," yelled Mal.

Uma laughed mischievously.

Mal wasn't the only one surprised to see Uma. "Uma!" shouted Harry and Gil in unison. The scallywags were excited to see their long-lost captain.

"That's my name," said Uma, still balancing the dying ember. She glowed with confidence and gave her friends a coy wave. Then she wrapped her tentacle tightly around the ember and sank into the dark water.

"No!" shrieked Mal. All was truly lost.

Uma's marvelous gold shell necklace brightened

beneath the waving sea. Then a whirling burst of water gushed upward out of the ocean's roiling surface, exploded, and rained back down on everyone who stood on the bridge. Mal and her friends were drenched. They scrambled to the side railing, expecting to see a tentacled Uma rise dramatically from the sea once more. But there was no sign of her.

"Hi, boys," said a voice behind them. Everyone spun around to see Uma on the Auradon side of the bridge, looking fabulous in her teen-girl form. She wore fish scale leggings and a pair of aqua cowboy boots with gold crustacean accents. Her clothes were beaded with shells and sea glass. In her hand was the still-lit ember.

Harry Hook sprang to the other side of the bridge. He circled his friend, a wicked smile on his face. "Welcome back," he said.

"Uma, you swam off and forgot all about us," said Gil, sounding a little hurt.

"Planning her revenge, no doubt." Mal stared at Uma.

"It's not all about you," said Uma. She'd felt bad

about leaving her minions leaderless, but she'd been gone for good reason. "I was looking for a hole in the barrier, to let everyone out. And you know what I found, boys?" Uma threw her arms wide and gestured toward Auradon and the open sea. "It's better out here than we thought. There's this thing that looks like a furry rock, called a coconut. And fish so big you could dance on their backs," said Uma. She pointed at Mal and her friends accusingly and snarled, "And they've been keeping it all for themselves."

Mal didn't have time to discuss all the ways poor little Shrimpy felt she'd been shorted in life. Audrey was gaining ground in Auradon while Mal stood there listening to the adventures of an octopus. "I need that ember to break a spell," she told Uma.

"Cast by Audrey, Sleeping Beauty's daughter," added Carlos, trying to help.

Uma lapped up this delicious news. "Oooh, the good guy's the bad guy. I might not give it back. See what happens."

The pirate captain soaked in the moment of power. She had something Mal desired. Now she just needed to decide how best to use that advantage.

Mal pleaded with Uma. "It's not the time for games," she said. "People's lives are in danger."

Uma looked at Auradon, the city that was shunning her, and back at Mal, the girl who had caused the shunning. Why should Uma care what happened to them? Weren't they the very same people who had booed her presence at Cotillion? Uma had made up her mind. "Guarantee me that every single villain kid who wants to get off the island can," she said.

"I can't do that," countered Mal.

"Well, how about now?" threatened Uma. She dangled the still-lit ember over the bridge's railing, determined to get what she wanted. Enough of this four-at-a-time application process; if Mal wanted the ember, every last villain kid was getting released from their Isle sentence.

Mal looked back and forth among the dangling ember, the girl she called Shrimpy, and Auradon City. She made a choice.

"Deal," Mal said, knowing she couldn't possibly keep that promise. "Deal," she repeated.

Uma eyed Mal skeptically. She had no reason to believe her rival was telling the truth.

Evie jumped in. "Uma, her word is good."

Mal flinched, pained by the knowledge that she'd lied to Evie as well.

Uma looked hard at Evie's sincere expression and honest eyes, then opened her gold shell necklace, placed the ember within it, and sealed it away safely. "I'll still keep this for the time being. 'Cuz if you think I trust you to save the world on your own, think again." Uma smiled and looked toward Harry and Gil. "This is a job for pirates!" she exclaimed.

Harry and Gil rushed Uma, and together the wretched threesome hooted and roared in triumphant reunion.

Mal grimaced, appalled at the prospect of joining forces with a gang of double-crossing pirates. Jay leaned in and said what they both were thinking. "We can always go back to hating each other when it's over."

"Fine," she said, standing with arms crossed.

Agreement reached, Jay went to Harry and Gil with a menacing stride. They had business to settle. "Where are our bikes?"

"Oh yeah," said Gil. "We crashed them." He smiled oafishly at the memory of it.

Harry pantomimed the bikes vrooming along, then meeting a fiery end. How he loved taunting Jafar's son.

Evie interrupted brightly. "Here's a thought. We could try being friends. Put our history behind us and celebrate our differences. Yeah?" She pulled out her red wristlet, which contained several blue spheres, and jingled it. "Who wants gum?" she asked optimistically.

Everyone stared at Evie in great confusion. Had she seriously just tried to mend fences with gum?

"Let's go," Uma ordered Harry and Gil.

"Uh, no," Mal said, stopping her. "I'm in charge." She paused, then gave her own order to the group. "Let's go."

With that, the strangely united band of villains started the long walk across the bridge toward Auradon.

CHAPTER FIFTEEN

FALLING ASLEEP DURING CLASS—TOTALLY NORMAL. EVERYONE DOES IT. WELL, AT LEAST I DID IT. BUT DURING LUNCH? NOW THAT'S FREAKY.

The motley crew of villain kids marched over the bridge, hiked along the craggy coast, and wound their way up the road that led to Auradon Prep. The scene that greeted them was shocking. The school's green lawn was littered with sleeping students.

"They're asleep—everyone," said Evie, absorbing the alarming sight.

Mal, Evie, Jay, and Carlos tried their cell phones, hoping to reach someone who could provide an explanation, but not one of them worked.

"I can't get Ben," said Mal, worried.

"Or Dizzy or Doug," Evie added with concern.

"Or Jane. Signal's out," confirmed Carlos.

Celia wandered ahead of the group, turning her head from side to side every few feet. There was just so much to look at. Her jaw fell open when she spotted the most enormous building she'd ever seen. "Is that Auradon Prep?"

"Yeah, and when everybody wakes up, you're going to love it," Carlos said with a smile.

"Yes!" exclaimed Celia. With everything that had happened, she'd almost forgotten about getting to go to school. In Auradon. In that beautiful building.

Gil, too, stood in awe of Auradon Prep, which until that moment had been a place he'd only heard about. The lush gardens, the chirping birds, the manicured lawns—it was all more than he had imagined. "It's all so . . ."

"Freaky," offered Jay. It disturbed him to see so many of his classmates spelled into hibernation.

"Green!" corrected Gil, his eyes as big as saucers. "You have leaves on your trees. And what are those colorful things in your bushes?"

"Uh. Flowers," Jay answered quizzically.

"Flowers are pretty," Gil gushed. Then his eyes fell on the prettiest sight yet: a large bowl of ripe red grapes that sat atop a picnic table, left unfinished by a sleeping eater. "Cantaloupes!" he shouted, and pounced on the snack. Gil put his hands around the large bowl, lifted it to his mouth, and dumped the whole bunch of grapes in at once. He broke out in a huge dopey grin. What Gil lacked in brains he made up for in pure joy.

Uma raised her eyebrows. "We don't have any fresh fruit on the Isle, remember?" she said in explanation.

Jay leaned into Gil and patted him on the back. "They're grapes," he explained kindly.

"Grapes." Gil rolled the word over his tongue. "Love grapes," he said definitively.

As Gil chewed happily on the sleeping student's lunch, Harry sashayed up to another napper and picked his pocket. It wasn't like the sleeping kid was spending his money.

"I believe I deserve compensation for my muscles, my wiles, my role in this endeavor," said Harry, surveying the dozing crowd and deciding which sleeper to steal from next.

Jay flexed his arms threateningly and pounded his right fist into his left palm. "You do: me not squashing you like a bug." He grabbed the cash from Harry's hook, shook his head, and put it back.

Harry held his sharp hook to Jay's throat. "Think I'm scared of you, Jay?"

Jay stuck his face inches from Harry's and was about to speak when Mal and Uma noticed their first lieutenants battling egos. "Guys," snapped the impatient leaders in unison. Both girls were surprised by their moment of solidarity.

Nearby, Carlos did a double take and broke out in a huge smile. Was that . . . No, it couldn't be.

"Mmmmm, delicious," said a familiar voice.

"Dude?" Carlos cried.

Dude sat beneath a picnic table, eating a hot dog from a conked-out boy's hand. The mutt was living his best life. Dude looked up, caught in the act, and belched.

"Dude, really?" asked Carlos, trying to stifle a laugh.

"He wasn't eating it," the dog barked drily.

Carlos realized the dog might have some answers. "Dude, do you know what happened here?"

"Yeah, Audrey put everybody to sleep. Oh, and then she turned some of them—"

"Guys!" cried Evie. She pointed at a statuesque girl who stood a few feet away from Dude. "Hannah's turned to stone." Hannah was frozen in granite, still wearing her marching band uniform.

"All right, everyone stay on their toes," warned Jay, looking out for the group. The sleeping kids, the stone students—it was all Audrey's doing. She had to be stopped.

"Look, since we're here, let's check the school," suggested Uma. Harry, Celia, and Gil followed her toward the entrance.

"No," said Mal, flanked by Evie, Carlos, and Jay. She spoke with authority. "Audrey went straight for the crown, so I think it's safe to assume she's going to go for Ben and his castle next. That's where we'll go."

"Says who?" asked Uma, stepping up to Mal.

"Says me." Mal leaned toward the girl she called Shrimpy.

"Says you and that's supposed to mean something to me?" asked Uma. She was not about to take orders from Mal.

"Guys," implored Evie. They had bigger fish to fry. Not that Uma was frying fish anymore. They just had more important matters to focus on, like stopping Audrey.

Uma acquiesced . . . this time.

"To the castle," said Mal, satisfied with her small victory.

CHAPTER SIXTEEN

TAKE IT FROM ME: THAT WHOLE KNIGHT-IN-SHINING-ARMOR THING? IT'S WAY OVERRATED.

The idyllic Fairy Cottage lay hidden deep in the forest in the middle of a beautiful glade with trees that grew high into the sky. Its whimsical rubblestone chimney, wood-framed windows, and overgrown English garden lent to the cabin's peaceful feel.

The quaint cottage that had once hidden Aurora from Maleficent now had a new resident: Audrey. She stood inside the cheery cottage, among the winsome lace curtains and hand-embroidered wall art, and threw a colossal fit.

With untamed fury, she stared into the orb of Maleficent's scepter. The magical glass sphere showed Mal, Jay, and the rest of the squad making their way through the streets of Auradon City. Audrey was livid. "How did Mal break my spell?" Audrey screamed. The china teacups that lined the shelves shook with reverberations.

Chad shrugged innocently. "I don't know," he said.

"And what is Uma doing here?" Audrey asked. She turned over a glass fruit bowl, emptied the green apples onto the frilly tablecloth, and chucked the bowl in Chad's direction. Chad ducked nimbly out of the way and fretted. Perhaps he'd made a mistake, joining forces with Audrey. She was out of control.

"Come clean, Chad. Where did they go?" she asked, menacing.

Chad flinched and inched toward the cottage door. "I don't know. I could go check for you," he offered, hoping to escape Audrey's mounting wrath.

"Stay," boomed Audrey as she tightened her fingers around the scepter.

Chad slumped his shoulders and silently obeyed. Audrey walked toward her little pet and ran her fingers through his hair. She grinned malevolently and turned her attention back to the scepter's orb and the image of Mal and her friends approaching Ben's palace. "It's about to get a little ugly."

Audrey watched as Mal ran down the grand palace hall, followed closely by the other seven travelers. "Ben could be asleep anywhere," Mal said, worried.

"Or turned to stone," Celia managed to squeak out before Evie clamped her hand over Celia's mouth.

"Ben," yelled Mal. Her unanswered shouts echoed through the chamber.

Dude sniffed around. "I've got his scent. Very pungent cologne. Easy to track. Follow me."

"That's great, Dude," said Jay.

"FYI, I give great cuddles, too," the dog announced proudly.

Did someone say cuddles? Gil thought. His face lit up with glee. "Really? I never had a pet except for the elk head in my dad's man cave," he said.

Uma stared thoughtfully at a series of deep claw marks scratched into the wall. She ran her finger over them. "What's this?" A framed ancient map that hung on the wall had been cut clean in half.

"Any chance that was already there?" asked Carlos.

He looked around the room nervously. The royal-blue curtains were tattered and torn, and the mysterious scratches continued along the corridor for many feet.

"Follow me," Dude offered, then led the group out of the room and toward the scent he'd detected.

Moments later, the group trailed Dude into the palace's hall of armor. Sunlight shone through the domed stained glass ceiling, illuminating artwork of the great battle scenes and gallant knights of past reigns. The group approached the grand foyer with great reverence. Silver swords with glistening blades and shields battered from combat hung on the wood-paneled walls. Foreboding suits of armor that had been collected through the ages stood stiffly on platforms.

As the villain squad crept through the majestic hall, Harry inspected all the tempting treasures. His eyes lingered on the more portable items, like a sparkling halberd and antique shield, and he wondered if anyone would notice if a few trinkets mysteriously went missing. He was a pirate, after all, and looting came naturally. As if reading his mind, Jay moved up quietly behind Harry. "I can feel you lurking," Harry told Jay without needing to turn around.

"Good," said Jay. He pushed Harry along. Not trusting the seasoned villain, Jay vowed to keep a close eye on him.

They weren't the only members of the two feuding villain cliques to clash. Carlos had had just about enough of Gil, who had taken an intense liking to Dude. "So you can track, cuddle, and talk? Do you think your puppies would be able to talk, too?" Gil asked, scratching the dog under his chin.

"He's taken. If you want a dog, adopt a rescue," said Carlos possessively.

"Ha ha, talking puppies," mused Dude. He walked over to Celia to be scratched. "He seems nice," the chatty canine said, oblivious to Carlos's feelings.

Across the room, Uma and Mal were locked in their own tête-à-tête. "Bet you lost a little sleep thinking about me on the loose," Uma goaded Mal.

"Nah. Dragons don't really lose sleep," Mal countered. "I wonder what fried octopus tastes like," she added, just to annoy Uma.

Evie stepped between the two girls and threw her arms around their shoulders in a gesture of solidarity. "Okay, why don't we not do this?"

"We're celebrating our differences," Uma said sarcastically.

Clank! Clash! A suit of armor that had stood stiff for centuries on a high wood pedestal clicked its heels and turned toward the group.

"I believe we're being challenged," said Harry, his hook dancing in the air. Harry was always itching for a good fight.

Mal and Uma, too busy one-upping each other, failed to heed Harry's warning. "Let's all split up and look for Audrey," Uma told Mal.

Mal balked at Uma's suggestion. "That makes absolutely no sense. Unless I stop her with the ember, she'll spell you." Mal was unsure how much longer she could handle listening to this insipid pirate. Mal was in charge, not Uma.

Harry cleared his throat and interrupted the girls' competitive confab again. "We have a situation here," he alerted them. That would prove to be an understatement.

The bewitched knight moved and spoke ominously in Audrey's voice. The effect was disturbing. "You like a prince, Mal. How about a knight in shining armor? Or knights?" The lead knight swung his lethal sword with a swift, authoritative gesture, and the rest of the suits of armor in the long hall magically clinked to life and drew their sharpened swords on the VKs.

Uma and Mal shared a furtive look. Spooked and outnumbered, Mal, Uma, and their friends backed up, spun around, and rushed toward the hall exit. But before they could reach it, two menacing knights stepped forward and blocked the doors. Exiting would not be an option.

Gil grabbed two gleaming swords and handed one to Uma. Jay followed Gil's lead and snatched several swords, then tossed a blade to Mal with perfect precision. Harry snatched the halberd he'd been eyeing earlier. He had known he'd end up with the coveted treasure somehow.

Uma jumped up onto a tall platform in the center of the hall. "Fall back, let me lead," Uma shouted to the others.

Mal bristled. She would not be outranked by a puny, gutless pirate. Mal leapt onto the raised platform and, with a confident heft, lifted her sword above her head. This was her fight, her command, and they'd follow her battle plan. "Swords in the air if you're with me," Mal declared.

Uma did not comply. She flashed a fake grin, stepped in front of Mal, and whipped around her turquoise hair. She was not about to fall in line.

Evie looked askance at both girls, then jumped between them, planted her hands on her hips, and sternly reminded both sides that at the moment they were all on the same side. And they were gravely outnumbered. The only way to defeat Audrey's armor army was to set aside their differences—at least until the battle was done.

The enchanted knights marched with military precision and attacked the teens in one swift swoosh. Swords clanged, blades scraped, metal clashed against metal. Three towering soldiers yielding razor-sharp swords cornered Mal and Uma. Without thinking, the girls parried in sync and fought off the first two knights together. *Clink!* One knight. *Clank!* Another knight. The third knight lunged at Uma, his sword outstretched. With dragon-fast speed, Mal kicked his foot out from under him, which sent him stumbling to the ground with a crash. Uma looked up, surprised to see Mal was the one who'd had her back. Mal shrugged, then rejoined the melee. The battle raged on.

Mal jumped in next to Harry and Jay, who stood back to back, swerving and deflecting blows in a coordinated effort. Behind them, Carlos and Gil worked together, dashing and darting about, attempting to attack an indomitable knight from both sides.

Mal dueled with the lead knight, her bluish-purple hair flying behind her. Their swords collided midair with a shudder. The knight shifted his weight and gained advantage over Mal. Just in time, Uma yelped loudly and distracted the knight long enough for Mal to spin away. She turned and found herself standing face to face with yet another attacking knight. Mal groaned. The unyielding knights kept coming.

The unstoppable armor army was on its way to easily trouncing the band of VKs. Their swords moved so quickly they were a blur. Mal looked around the hall at her friends, who stumbled with exhaustion. They fought valiantly but were overwhelmed and overmatched. Mal's eyes flashed green with focus. She pushed through the chaos, made her way back up to the platform, and stared at the doomed battle scene below. With a confident, clear voice, she incanted: *"Suit of armor, strong and true, make this armor bust a move."* Then she raised her arms high and launched into a sick dance move. Having fallen under Mal's spell, the knights raised their swords and duplicated Mal's dance move, swaying their hips from side to side.

Catching on, Uma jumped onto the platform beside Mal. She popped it and pumped it, causing the seashells on her jacket to rattle. The knights repeated every one of her moves. Carlos, too, put the knights through a complex combination. Celia, not wanting to miss out on what now looked like fun, ran back into the hall and rejoined the others. The knights matched the teens' hip-hop moves step for step, and one by one, the metal soldiers exhausted themselves and dropped to the floor with a clatter, collapsing into a large heap of metal. The lead knight, last to fall, toppled with a deafening crash.

Exhilarated by victory, Mal and Uma forgot themselves. They smiled at each other and high-fived. Behind them, Jay and Harry chest-bumped while Gil and Carlos shared congrats. The moment was sweet until the two sides remembered they were supposed to be sworn enemies. The teens separated quickly into their two distinct cliques, abandoning any sign of friendship that had been there just moments before. Mal, Jay, and Carlos stood to one side, while Uma, Gil, and Harry stood to the other.

Only Evie jumped forward. "No. Guys, come on," she said. "This was so great. We were a team. We worked together. Come on, admit it."

Everyone glared at Evie in silence, but she remained undeterred. They'd already done the hard part of coming together; now they just had to acknowledge it.

"You know what we should try? An icebreaker. You say something you really like about the other person. I'll start." Evie turned to Harry and thoughtfully considered her options. "Harry. Great accent," she said. "Now you go."

Uma rolled her eyes and let out an exasperated breath. "Is she always this perky?"

"Oh, it wasn't your turn, but thank you," Evie gushed.

Mal turned to Evie and took both of her hands in hers. "Evie, I love you." Evie broke into a huge smile. "I love you, too." Her icebreaker was working—or maybe it wasn't.

Mal continued. "I love the energy, but we're very short on time. Audrey clearly knows we're here. And we need to get out of here ASAP."

"All right, where does this cheerleader bunk down?" asked Uma. "If she's not there, we might find some sort of clue."

"Actually, she's still in the dorm," offered Evie.

"You're right, because of summer school," said Mal.

"Summer school," Harry said, scrunching up his face in utter disgust. "No wonder she wants revenge."

Mal pointed to Jay, Carlos, Dude, Harry, and Gil.

"Okay, I need you guys to go find Ben. We will meet back at Evie's place in two hours."

"Sounds like we're going with my plan," boasted Uma. "Just sayin'."

"It was kinda the obvious plan," said Mal.

Gil piped up. "Uma said it first."

"Right, so my plan," Uma said, gratified. She high-fived Harry and Gil, proud of her small victory over Mal.

"Whatever!" Mal exclaimed, throwing her arms in the air as she headed out of the hall.

CHAPTER SEVENTEEN

EVERY VILLAIN HAS HER LAIR. IF I WERE SLEEPING BEAUTY'S DAUGHTER, WHERE WOULD I HIDE? AND YES, I KNOW MY MOTHER WOULD KNOW THE ANSWER TO THAT QUESTION. THAT HELPS ME HOW?

In Audrey's dorm room, Uma stretched out on the lavish bed and flipped through Audrey's journal. She leafed through the pages, reading the private thoughts Audrey had recorded in her loopy cursive handwriting. Ever since Mal arrived at Auradon Prep, Audrey had felt invisible at school. And at home, her family acted like she'd let them down. Uma scanned another page. Audrey was humiliated and heartbroken when Ben publicly declared his love for Mal. Uma had assumed Audrey was some privileged rich girl, but maybe it wasn't that simple.

Uma was absorbed in Audrey's journal when Mal and Evie ran into the room out of breath. "She's nowhere on campus," Evie panted. They'd checked the cafeteria, searched the tourney field, and even rummaged around in the library. Audrey had left a long trail of pink fog and sleeping students in her wake, but the sorceress herself had vanished.

"Found her diary," said Uma. "And dang, did you ruin Audrey's life."

Mal was starting to feel kind of bad. "Okay, so did you find anything in there we don't already know, or . . ."

"She hangs out at Fairy Cottage. You know, where Flora, Fauna, and Merryweather hid her mom from your mom," Uma told Mal. The pirate leader rubbed her hands together and hooted with evil glee.

"Yes, ha ha ha, the irony is not lost on me," said Mal.

Uma lifted her head from a poufy down pillow and ran her fingertips along the dreamy silk comforter. It was all so luxurious. "How could anyone with this bed ever be unhappy?" she wondered aloud. Kids on the Isle were lucky if they had a bale of hay to sleep on. Uma herself had spent many a night sleeping on the hard wood planks of her pirate ship.

Evie nodded silently and thought, *Note to self: every VK gets a great new pillow and comforter.* She added it to her long mental to-do list. Thanks to the future Queen Mal, Auradon would soon be home to every villain kid who wanted to live there. Evie smiled at the beautiful thought. Of course, there was so much to do to get ready for the new students to move into the dorms. Speaking of whom . . .

Celia had been busy pilfering through Audrey's vanity, and she swiveled around, proud to model her new image. "Okay, how do I look?" she asked, striking a pose. She wore several gold bangles, three strands of pearls, and Audrey's signature bluebird tiara. With Celia, more was more.

Evie looked her up and down. "Okay, the bling stays here," instructed Evie.

"But she's bad," Celia said, pouting.

"And we're not," replied Evie.

Celia removed the tiara with a disappointed sigh.

Mentoring all the young VKs who'd be moving from the Isle wasn't going to be easy, but there was nothing in the world Evie would rather do.

Meanwhile, Jay, Carlos, Harry, and Gil trudged down an overgrown path deep in the Auradon forest. They called out for Ben. Dude sniffed around the trees for any sign of the king. Gil, who was in his own little joy bubble, scarfed down tiny red berries directly off a bush. "These things grow everywhere," he said with doltish wonder, popping another one into his mouth. "Hey, we should play that icebreaker. Um, Jay, I like the way that you can bounce around and jump off things," he said with a mouthful of fruit and bright berry juice dripping down his chin.

After years of stealing rotting food from rickety stalls and foraging through dumpsters for dinner, Gil was in paradise. "This is free, right?" he asked, plucking off two more handfuls of berries.

Jay found Gil's attitude refreshing and decided to play his game. "Yeah. I like how you get a kick out of a berry bush," he told Gil.

Gil looked slightly embarrassed. "I guess you've

probably seen everything by now, huh? Furry rocks, giant fish. You're probably used to grabbing lunch off a bush."

Now it was Jay's turn to be a little embarrassed. "No—I mean, no, not really," he said. "I mean, I mainly just use the vending machines at practice. You know, tourney kind of eats up most of my time."

Harry snorted derisively. "Tourney? That's a wee boy's game."

Jay ignored him.

"You know what would be fun?" Gil said, looking out over Auradon dreamily. "To go rafting down a jungle river,"

"Find a lost civilization," said Jay, taking a shine to the idea. He'd been in Auradon a while but hadn't seen much of the country. He let the thought rattle around in his head as he grabbed a mouthful of berries. They were delicious.

"Or maybe a penguin," said Gil. He'd once seen a clip of the funny little birds while watching reruns on TV, and he liked how they wobbled.

"Well, you find those more on, like, icebergs," remarked Jay. "But I'd love to see one of those."

Harry found the cheery tone of their conversation sickening. He sauntered over and sneered. "You guys are killing me." The swashbuckler glided up to the bush and slowly picked a single berry with his glinting hook. He put it in his mouth, in what seemed like slow motion, and smiled. Much to his annoyance, Jay and Gil were right. The fruit was delicious.

Hoping to save face, Harry pointed his hook down a dark, shadowy forest path. "And PS: the mutt went thataway."

"Dude, what do you see?" shouted Carlos, running off. They had a king to find. Harry and Gil followed. But Jay hung back for a moment and returned to the simple berry bush. With a new sparkle in his eye, he picked one more. Something felt right about that small act of freedom.

Two hours later, Mal, Evie, and Uma hurried toward Evie's starter castle, ready to reunite with the boys as planned. Celia raced ahead.

"I hope they found Ben," said Mal, thinking of how happy she'd be to see him.

As they walked up the path, Uma eyed Evie's

picturesque castle. She was truly impressed. Evie hadn't inherited the home like the other spoiled little Auradon princesses Uma loathed. Evie's success was self-made, and Uma respected that. "Nice digs," said Uma, and she meant it.

"I got a really good deal," said Evie. She shrugged modestly and downplayed her good fortune for Uma's benefit.

Celia reached the front door first, threw it open, and bounded into Evie's living room. Her face fell when she spotted Squeaky and Squirmy tangled up in each other's arms, deep asleep on a comfy gray couch. Their glasses sat askew on their sweet slumbering faces.

Mal, Evie, and Uma took in the tragic scene. Evie's heart nearly broke when she saw innocent little Dizzy curled up on the other end of the couch. She was still dressed in her green-and-pink ruffled dress and vintage stone brooch, ready for a party she never got to attend. Instead, she tossed and turned from a bad dream.

Celia reached over and did her best to soothe her buddy. "Don't worry, Dizzy. We can fix this." She covered Dizzy with a soft red afghan. "And once we do, they're going to let all the kids come from the Isle. So happy dreams, okay?"

Evie and Uma smiled at each other, their hearts warmed by hearing their shared VK goal mentioned aloud. Mal looked away, her face covered by a veil of guilt.

The tender moment was cut short by a booming snore that sounded from the next room. The noise startled the wits out of all four girls. Uma followed the thundering sound through the doorway and stepped into Evie's glass work space, where she discovered Doug sprawled out on an imported area rug. "Who's the dude?" asked Uma.

Evie ran to Doug and shook him. "Doug. Wake up, wake up."

"He's spelled," said Uma. She turned to Mal, confused. "Is she not a fast learner?"

"She's emotionally involved, okay?" said Mal.

"In that case, she should be able to wake him up. True Love's Kiss? Works every time?" said Uma wryly. Her own plot to take over Auradon had been spoiled the past spring by one such kiss between Mal and Ben. The memory still smarted. Uma looked at Evie expectantly and braced herself for the mushy moment.

Evie diverted her eyes. "We haven't actually used the L-word yet," she confessed bashfully.

Uma raised her eyebrows. This was going to be good.

Evie looked at Doug adoringly. His head rested on a shagged pillow; his right arm was folded behind his head. She placed her hand affectionately on Doug's forehead, as if ready to wake him with a kiss. Then she furrowed her brow in a self-conscious expression and straightened back up quickly.

"Can we be alone?"

Uma and Mal exchanged knowing looks, walked out, and shut the door behind them. Then they immediately popped their heads back around the carved-wood doorway to watch. As if they were about to miss the big kiss!

Evie looked at Doug in abject panic. She cared about Doug more than anything. He was kind-hearted and funny, and his unwavering belief in Evie was something she'd never experienced before. For

Evie, Doug was definitely the one. She thought they both felt the same, but she didn't know for sure. They'd never actually talked about it. *Does he love me, does he not? Do I love him? Is it strong enough?* she thought.

What if she kissed him, a real True Love's Kiss, and he didn't wake up? She couldn't bear the thought. But this was Doug and her, and they were perfect together. She stepped outside to think.

With a burst of realization, Evie flew back inside to Doug and kissed him on the lips. But Doug didn't wake from the spell—or so it seemed. Behind his glasses, Doug opened one green eye, then shut it sneakily, in hopes of getting another kiss.

Evie caught him in the act and playfully swatted his knee. She tried to stay mad but couldn't. The kiss settled it. What Doug and Evie shared was definitely true love.

Mal smiled at her two friends, super happy for them. Then she looked at the clock with concern. Jay and the guys should have been there by then. She frowned and hoped they hadn't run into trouble.

CHAPTER EIGHTEEN

WHO KNEW MY PERFECTLY REGAL BOYFRIEND HAD A WILD SIDE? I LIKE IT....

Jay, Carlos, Gil, Harry, and Dude walked through the woods in search of Ben.

"Ben," shouted Carlos. His call echoed through the tall trees.

Dude heard a rustling sound coming from a patch of trees and paused. "Woo, boy, you've got to be smelling that, right?" He stuck his little wet nose in the air.

Without warning, a terrible beast with wild eyes, matted fur, and a booming roar burst out from behind the trees.

Each of the four boys raised his fists (or hook) in a defensive stance, ready to fight the brute. The beast lunged toward Harry, but Jay quickly pulled the pirate out of the way.

Harry studied the untamed creature that growled in front of him. Granted, he hadn't been in Auradon very long, but he knew a king when he saw one—and this was not it. The pirate looked pointedly at Dude. "You need some serious nose adjustments," he critiqued.

Carlos stepped forward tentatively to take a closer look at the feral creature. The beast had familiar eyes. "Ben?" Carlos asked.

The beast turned toward Carlos and nodded his enormous furry head.

"Huh, I thought I recognized those pants," said Jay, noting the beast's blue racing pants with yellow side stripes. The outfit looked familiar, with one notable difference: the pants now sported a large hole in back, through which the beast's long bushy tail whipped around wildly.

The beast clawed his way up a dirt mound, clutched his large paw, and roared with monstrous pain.

"Aw, he's got a boo-boo," said Gil. "That's why

he's so cranky. You know, my dad said his dad did not handle pain well. At all."

Beast Ben let out a deafening and dangerous-sounding growl, drew back his massive arm, and took a savage swipe at Gil.

Jay looked at Carlos. "You're good with animals. Do something."

"What? Okay . . ." Carlos took a deep calming breath and approached the untamed brute with cautious steps. "Hey, Ben. It's me, Carlos, all right?"

The beast snarled, bared his teeth, and launched toward Carlos.

"Whoa, whoa, Ben, it's me, Carlos. You know me." Carlos reached for the beast's injured paw. The creature snatched it back with a deep, intimidating howl.

"You helped me once. Remember, with Dude? Let me help you. Let me see your hand," said Carlos tenderly.

The beast relaxed and reluctantly held out his paw. A large gnarly splinter was stuck in his palm, the flesh around it puckered angrily.

Carlos looked from the nasty wound to the beast's

pointy teeth and hesitated. Jay nodded at Carlos with confidence; he could do this.

"Let's count. One, two, three." Carlos gently grabbed the splinter with both hands, tugged, and removed the offending wood shaving from the beast's palm. With the piercing pain gone, the beast released a deafening roar of relief.

"There it is. You did it!" said Carlos. It was unclear if he was talking to the beast or to himself.

Out of nowhere, a forceful stream of water blasted the terrifying beast in the chest. All heads turned to find Jane standing in the forest clearing, looking intrepid and no-nonsense. She aimed Chad's water gun at the beast and squirted him with a rapid-fire stream of water from the Enchanted Lake.

Carlos and Jane locked eyes and wasted no time in sprinting toward each other. They hugged happily and talked over each other in excitement. "When you didn't show up, I was sure she got you, too," said Jane, taking Carlos's hand.

"I was so worried. I didn't forget your party. We had to go and I forgot to call," said Carlos earnestly.

"I'm so glad you're all right!" exclaimed Jane and

Carlos in unison. They giggled. The reunion was nothing short of adorable.

Ben looked at Jane with great appreciation. He was soaking wet, but he was King Ben again.

"All right, you good?" asked Jay, helping Ben down from the mound. "Take a seat right there," he said, pointing toward a sizable tree trunk.

"Yeah, uh-huh." Ben still seemed a bit shaken up. "That was funky."

"Was. Is," said Jay, tilting his head and staring at Ben. Ben still looked part beast, with unruly hair, a full beard, and teeth pointy enough to be called fangs.

"You need another blast," Jane said decidedly with a knowledgeable nod.

Carlos beamed at Jane proudly: that smart girl thought of everything.

Jane raised the sprayer to waist level, cocked it with confidence, and blasted Ben with more water, this time to no effect. He was still beast-ish. "Please stop," said Ben, water dripping down his face.

Jane emptied the water gun with one final useless squirt. "Huh. It's Enchanted Lake water. But I guess there's only so much it can do."

Harry watched the scene from afar and was impressed by the bubbly girl. "Well, well, well," he said, sauntering up to Jane. He bowed low in an exaggerated gentlemanly fashion. "Harry Hook. And you, my little duckling, are ravishing."

"Ravishing and taken," said Carlos emphatically as he tried to stand tall. "Just in case anyone was confused." He stepped right between Jane and Harry and shot the pirate the meanest look he could manage, then made a point of putting his other arm around Jane. Jane's bright blue eyes danced with excitement. Carlos had just called her ravishing.

Ben listened to the exchange with great confusion. "Hold on. Whose side are they on?" asked Ben, baffled. The last time he'd seen Harry, the nasty pirate had him roped to a ship mast and was ordering him to walk the plank. The king was not a fan.

Jay did his best to catch Ben up on the day's events, but it was difficult. An unfathomable number of things had gone down in just a few short hours. "They escaped and joined us. Mal has the ember, which is our only hope to stop Audrey. Details to follow," said Jay.

"Hades's ember? Has Mal gone back to the Isle?" Ben asked. He was utterly perplexed.

"I said 'details to follow'! We're meeting up with Mal, Evie, and Uma," Jay told Ben.

"Uma?" Ben's mouth hung agape and his eyes widened in shock. Ben couldn't imagine how she had ended up in the mix.

The whole group leveled looks at Ben. *"Details to follow,"* everyone yelled in unison.

As they set off through the woods, Harry looked at Jay, tipped his hat, then ran his hook slowly over his chin and grinned. "Hey, Jay, um . . ." The pirate cleared his throat awkwardly. "Thanks for saving me gorgeous face." He swatted Jay on the back in an almost-friendly way.

CHAPTER NINETEEN

Here's the thing: I'm not ready to have a slumber party where we braid each other's hair or anything, but I guess Uma can be kinda cool.

Uma and Celia sat in Evie's blue kitchen chairs with the pink cardboard bakery box between them. They each had a tall glass of milk and chowed down on slices of Jane's birthday cake.

Mal glanced out the window anxiously. "That was a good idea to check out Audrey's room. Now we know we're on track," she said. Perhaps she'd underestimated Ursula's daughter. After all, the girl had been successfully captaining a pirate crew for years.

"Is there an insult in there that I missed?" asked Uma as she lifted her fork to her mouth. The cake really was delicious.

"Just . . . I wanted to thank you," Mal said sincerely.

Uma was honestly touched.

Audrey stood in Fairy Cottage, watching Mal and Uma through the orb. She was disgusted by what she saw. Mal and Uma were getting along. They were . . . what? Becoming friends? Audrey was infuriated. "Think you're on the right track? You're not going anywhere," she taunted them. Then she turned to Chad, who stood quaking by her side. "Ugh. Let's mess them up."

Chad had other, less-evil ideas. "I say we go to my place and maybe binge-watch some TV. Or maybe order some stuff online," he suggested.

Audrey was unimpressed with the quivering fool. She swept her arm in a downward motion, and Chad groveled before her.

"What about pizza?" he asked.

Audrey thrust her scepter in his direction. Chad flinched in fear. "Oh, okay, you don't like pizza. Then, salad?"

Audrey stared at Chad for a beat before magically

blasting him back with a swift wave of her arms. "No saaaallllaaad," yelped Chad, but it was too late. He flew the length of the kitchen, directly into the open pantry, where he landed with a thud. The pantry door slammed and its wood bar fell into place, locking Chad securely inside among the sad sacks of flour and hanging dry herbs. He called for help, but his effort was futile. Audrey lifted her scepter high into the air. With Chad out of the way, she turned her wicked attention back toward Uma and Mal.

Mal and Uma were sitting together at Evie's kitchen table, genuinely enjoying each other's company.

"I maybe kinda missed the boat a little bit when I called you Shrimpy and wouldn't let you in the gang," Mal admitted, helping herself to a fingerful of frosting.

"Yeah, we could have really torn up the Isle together—" said Uma.

She was cut short by a loud slam. The girls jumped in alarm as a wood plank smacked into place across the kitchen window. *Slam! Slam! Slam!* The girls gasped and watched in fright as solid wood planks slammed one after another across every window and blocked out all but a crack of light.

Celia ran down the stairs and tried to throw open the front door, but several wood planks pounded mightily into place and sealed the exit. "We're trapped," she said. Celia backed away from the door and joined Mal and Uma in the center of the room. She was frightened. When Celia had first applied to Auradon Prep, she'd imagined a carefree life filled with too much sunshine, dorky pep rallies, and the opportunity to read the fortunes of wealthy Auradon Prep students—not lethal knights and magically sealed exits. This was not what she had bargained for.

Evie and Doug ran into the living room. "Are you guys okay? What's going on?" asked Evie, frightened. Her room, too, had been boarded up. Doug took Evie's hand and held it tightly.

Mal's eyes gleamed with frustration and anger. She'd had enough of Audrey's nastiness. She raised both of her hands and incanted from deep within her heart: *"You've caused my friends pain and fear. We've had enough. Now disappear."*

The planks merely rattled in response. That was not the result Mal was hoping for.

"You guys, I'm sorry," Mal told her friends. "My spells aren't working. Audrey's magic is getting stronger."

Uma stared down at her gold shell necklace, which now glowed with light. She had an idea. To Mal's surprise, Uma stepped forward to stand alongside her and grabbed her hand. Mal's eyes glowed green, Uma's necklace shone blue, and together the girls incanted: *You've caused our friends pain and fear. We've had enough. Now disappear.*

In a flash, the planks dislodged.

The girls stared at each other, amazed by their accomplishment.

"You did it. Together. This is what I've been talking about," cried Evie as she threw her arms around both girls.

"I guess my shell likes you," Uma said to Mal. Then she looked down at her necklace, opened the shell, and took out Hades's ember. She offered it to Mal as a token of trust. "Why don't you hang on to this?"

Mal nodded gratefully and accepted the ember. Celia looked out the open door and cheered with delight as their friends paraded up the front path to Evie's house, Ben in tow. "Hey, it's your bae," she told Mal.

Mal broke from the group, sprinted down the stone path to Ben, and flew into her fiancé's arms. "You okay?" asked Ben as he touched her cheek.

"A lot better now," Mal said, and hugged Ben tightly.

Ben looked over Mal's shoulder and spotted Uma. His eyes lit up, and he broke into a huge grin. "I always knew you'd be part of the solution," he said. Mal affectionately rested her hands on Ben's chest and nodded in agreement.

The kids greeted each other joyfully, glad to be reunited. Jane and Carlos hugged Celia, Jay put his arms around Evie and Doug, and Harry enveloped Uma. Meanwhile, Gil helped himself to a fresh orange off Evie's tree.

Mal ran her hand across Ben's scruffy beard and through his messy mane. "What is this?" she asked flirtatiously.

"You like this?" asked Ben with a glimmer in his eyes.

"Oh, yeah," said Mal. "I could get used to this. I love this." Her engagement ring caught the sun's rays as she tugged at her fiancé's whiskers.

"What about those?" asked Uma, pointing out Ben's sharp fangs.

Mal's wide-eyed reaction clearly read *Not so much.* "No," she said emphatically.

"I like 'em," admitted Ben with an impish grin.

Mal turned back to Ben and placed her hand on his arm. As much as she'd have loved to spend the afternoon just staring into his gorgeous eyes, they had an evil maniac to vanquish. "Okay, so we all think that Audrey could be at Fairy Cottage. We have no idea where it is. Did she ever take you there?"

Ben gritted his teeth at the memory of the grating afternoons he'd spent there. "Every Fairy Godmother's Day. Where's Fairy Godmother when you need her?"

Everyone looked toward Jane, who was seated quietly at a small white bistro table. She straightened her romper and clasped her hands together tensely. "I wish I knew." She looked away with worry but smiled when she saw Carlos standing next to her holding a small red box with a black-and-white polka-dot bow.

"Hey, um, this might be a bad time," he said, pulling up a seat next to her, "but happy birthday." He handed her the package. He'd been waiting for that moment all day. "I made it with my 3-D printer," he added hesitantly.

Jane carefully opened the box. She pulled out a gold necklace with a little pink accent bow and stared at it with wonder. The word *Jarlos*, written in beautiful gold script letters, hung in the middle of the chain.

"It's, uh, our names put together," Carlos babbled nervously.

"No, right, I get it," said Jane. She smiled awkwardly.

"Because we're together. You and me, we're like a couple," explained Carlos.

Jane's face radiated joy when she heard the word *couple*. "Right! 'Cuz Jane and Carlos makes Jarlos," said Jane.

"Yes, yeah! I could have gone with Cane. But I

went with Jarlos, unless you prefer Cane. Do you prefer Cane?"

"Oh, no, I love it!" exclaimed Jane. Her face glowed.

"You know what? I could remake it. It's cool, it's fine," he said, fumbling for words.

"No, Carlos," said Jane, rising from her seat. "It's perfect." Jane pulled back her long, dark glossy hair so Carlos could fasten the necklace around her neck. It was, by far, the most thoughtful and romantic gift Jane had ever received.

Ben hated to interrupt the intimate moment, but trouble was still brewing in Auradon. He set forth a plan. "Doug, go with Jane. We need to find Fairy Godmother."

Uma sized up Doug skeptically and shook her head in doubt. "They might need some muscle."

"Hey," yelped Doug defensively as he pushed up his glasses.

"Well, I'll go," Gil volunteered eagerly. He flexed his fit arms for good measure.

Carlos took Jane's hand in his. "Yeah, actually, I'd feel better."

"Yeah, actually, I'd feel better, too," Evie said.

"Same," chimed in Mal.

Doug puffed up his chest, tried to match Gil's brawn, and shrugged. "Yeah, actually, I would, too," he said, laughing.

Gil threw his thick arm around Doug and gave him a brotherly squeeze. "All right, man. Let's do it. Let's go, Jane."

"Be careful," said Carlos.

Mal put her head on Ben's shoulder as she watched the group take off down the path. Then she and the others turned to go back into Evie's house to plot their next steps. They had to stop Audrey . . . somehow.

CHAPTER TWENTY

AUDREY'S DARK POWER KEEPS GETTING STRONGER. I CAN'T SIT AROUND WAITING FOR HAPPILY EVER AFTER TO JUST HAPPEN. I SCREWED UP. NOW I HAVE TO MAKE THIS RIGHT.

Deep in the harrowing woods, the group silently approached Fairy Cottage and fanned out like a precision security team. Ben, Evie, and Mal hid behind a tree, while Jay, Carlos, and Harry positioned themselves near a large boulder. Uma and Celia brought up the rear. Mal removed the glowing ember from her pocket. She looked at it with determined eyes. This was the moment they'd been preparing for. It was time to stop Audrey once and for all.

Ben and Mal reached the flower-covered front gate, then signaled the others. With a collective whoosh of energy, the pirates and VKs rushed the house at once. The teens swooped through the front door, all ready to pounce.

Jay ran up the stairs in hopes of finding the dark princess but returned alone. "She's not upstairs," he said. The house was empty. Audrey was nowhere in sight.

A panicked pounding came from the kitchen cupboard. Ben ran to the kitchen, heaved open the weighty pantry door, and found a cowering Chad blubbering inside. "Chad?"

The once-charming prince was a total mess. "I want my mommy," Chad whimpered tearfully.

"What happened, buddy?" Ben asked, helping his friend up.

"Ben!" Chad startled. "Your face," he said, taking in the king's scruff. Then he looked at everyone else and noticed one important person missing. "She's gone! And the door's open. I'm free." He bolted out the front door and ran for freedom. Harry couldn't stop laughing at the cowardly prince.

Mal and Evie shared a knowing glance as Chad bolted past them. Not much *there* there. Mal looked around the cottage, irked that Audrey had managed to evade them again. She hoped the others were having more luck with their quest.

On the other side of town, Jane, Doug, and Gil strode through the Auradon Museum of Cultural History's grounds in search of Fairy Godmother. They finally discovered her on the back steps. "Oh my gosh, my mom has turned to stone, too," Jane said.

Tears welled up in Jane's wide eyes as she took in the sight. Doug put his arm around her supportively. Gil was sweet and gave her a reassuring nod. She scrunched her face, gathered her courage, and bravely approached her mother.

Jane was unsure of the proper thing to do, so she just started talking to her mom and hoped her heartfelt words would somehow cut through. "Hi, Mom. I don't know if you can hear me, Mom, but it's been a really crazy day. On the plus side, it's been the longest birthday I've ever had. On the minus side, everybody's under an evil spell. But on the plus side"—Jane paused, raised her hand to her chest, ran her fingers over her Jarlos necklace, and smiled broadly—"Carlos remembered my birthday, see." In that sense, it had been her best birthday yet.

Jane turned toward her mom with revitalized confidence. "We're going to figure out how to undo this. We'll find a way to make this right."

Back in the woods, Mal and her friends exited Fairy Cottage as dusk fell. "Okay, let's get this Audrey chick taken care of already," said Uma. Together, she and Mal should be able thwart the girl, no problem. And when they did, every VK on the Isle would get their freedom.

Uma looked at Mal. "What do you say, girl? Ready to wrap this up?" She and Mal fist-bumped.

Ben marveled at the newfound unity. He didn't know how it had happened, but he was delighted that it had. "Someday you're going to have to tell me how you guys all got teamed up."

Evie smiled brightly. "Actually, Mal promised to let all the kids off the Isle once this is over."

Ben was taken aback. He glanced at Mal searchingly.

Mal stared back at him, her eyes full of pain and guilt. She drew a deep breath, hesitated, then decided to come clean. She turned to face her friends and also face the truth. "I have to tell you all something. I lied to you," Mal said. "The kids won't be coming off the Isle." Mal felt ill just saying the words.

Jay shifted his weight and cocked his head in confusion. "What do you mean?"

Mal steeled her resolve before answering. There was no easy way to explain, especially to her friends. But she couldn't lie any longer. The other VKs needed to know the truth. "The program is shut down," she told them. "And the barrier will be closed for good."

The villain kids were stunned. Carlos looked bewildered. Evie stared at Mal, feeling raw and confused. Uma shot Mal the evil eye; she knew she never should have put her faith in that two-timing dragon.

Ben cleared his throat. "For Auradon's safety," he added, trying to explain. It didn't help.

"Hold up," Uma said, throwing her hands into the air, disappointment coating her voice. "So we're saving your precious people and your behinds for a

168

lie. I knew it was a mistake to trust you. You're always out for yourself."

Harry twirled his hook menacingly in the air. "And you? King Ben, eh? You're probably just going to throw us back inside, too." Ben detected a surprising sadness in Harry's eyes.

Celia marched right up to Mal and confronted her. "You know what? I actually thought you were brave, but you're just a chicken. Too scared to tell me I was never going to see my dad again," she raged. Tears of disillusionment filled her brown eyes.

Upset and let down, Celia grabbed the precious ember out of Mal's hand and threw it into a nearby birdbath. The mighty ember hissed and died out on the water, extinguished for good. Everyone gasped.

"No!" cried Mal. She rushed to rescue the ember as Celia whipped around her head of curls and ran away down the forest path.

"Celia," Evie yelled after her. The forest at night was no place for a young girl to wander around alone.

Mal reached into the birdbath and frantically pulled out the ember. Its spark was gone. Desperate,

Mal waved her fingers and attempted to relight it with a spell. She incanted: *"Regain your might and ignite."* Nothing happened. The ember sat still and dark.

Mal looked to Uma for help, but Uma was no longer interested in a dragon-octopus collab. The double-crossing villain would be walking the plank if she were on Uma's ship. But here, the best Uma could do was simply walk away.

"Bummer," Uma said to Mal, twirling her shell necklace in her hand. She turned to Harry. "Let's go find Gil and leave them all to rot." She snapped her fingers, then strode down the path away from Mal and everything she represented. Harry waved his hook with a flourish, pivoted on his heel, and followed Uma. The pirates were out of there.

"Uma," Mal cried after her.

Mal's friends looked at her in dismay. Jay's handsome face turned down as he tried to process the news. Carlos's puppy dog eyes were filled with pure disappointment. Evie just shook her head at Mal, crushed by her friend's deceit. The four of them were a team. How could Mal do this? How could she abandon their dream?

Evie's scorching look of condemnation hit Mal hard. "Evie, I'm so sorry. I'm sorry, I just . . . I was afraid to tell you. I thought I was going to lose my best friend. But I had to do something. I had to protect Auradon."

Evie drew her hands to her hips. "Closing the barrier was your idea?" Evie couldn't comprehend how Mal, of all people, could shut down the very program that had brought the four of them to Auradon. She'd forsaken everything they stood for.

Mal was desperate for her friends to understand. "I did it for us. I did it for our life that we have here now," she explained.

"For our life here? What about the kids we left behind on that island?" asked Evie, in tears. "The kids we promised. We were their only hope. I thought you were going to stand up for all the VKs. But instead you lied to them. And you lied to Jay. And you lied to Carlos. And you lied to me. We're your family."

"Evie, c'mon. I had no choice," pleaded Mal. If they could all just see it from her perspective . . .

In that moment, there was a flash of lightning; then Ben, Evie, Jay, Carlos, and Dude had all been turned to stone. Audrey's telltale fog swirled and billowed at their feet.

"Oh, no," Mal cried, her voice trembling with despair.

Mal's friends couldn't reply. They just stared at her with frozen expressions of hurt, disappointment, and betrayal. Mal gazed at the cold dark ember in her hand and realized all was lost. She was wrought with unbearable guilt.

Audrey's voice boomed overhead. "Now you're all alone, just like I was. . . ."

Despondent, Mal wondered how this all had happened. And deep inside, she knew the answer. She had to face herself and the lies she had chosen to tell and make it right. Yes, sometimes being a leader meant making unpopular decisions. But a true leader didn't deceive others about those decisions. Mal headed off through the forest, toward Auradon Prep, hoping to right the wrongs she'd set in motion.

A short while later, Mal bolted onto campus and saw Uma and Harry crossing the rear quad. Mal scrambled to catch up with them. "Uma, stop. Please stop.

I need your help. We have a chance if we do this together."

"Your friends kick you to the curb?" Uma glowered at her. "Good." She let out a *hmph* and kept walking.

Mal reached out to Uma again. "Ben saw something in you. And today, Uma, I saw it, too. You care, Uma. You care about everybody. Auradon is still worth saving. Help me, please," Mal implored her.

Uma paused and for a moment seemed to consider Mal's words. Then Harry stepped in. "You talk pretty, but she's made up her mind."

Uma's face set in a hardened expression. "You brought this on yourself, Mal. You figure out how to fix it."

The two pirates pushed past Mal, who was left standing alone, the consequence of her own bad choices. Under the bright moonlight, Mal dug deep, reflected, and realized the only happily ever after she'd see would be the one she wrote herself. Mal would have to fly higher—literally.

A hair-raising lightning bolt ripped through the sky over Auradon Prep. "Help me, Mal," cried a voice from above. *Wait a second,* Mal thought. *That was Celia's voice.*

Mal raised her eyes and saw Audrey's commanding silhouette atop the school's parapet. How had Audrey gotten Celia? When? She must have nabbed the girl from the forest, knowing Mal would come after her.

Mal's eyes flashed green and she disappeared in a cloud of purple smoke. Dragon Mal rose ferociously out of the smoke. It was time to put an end to Audrey's reign of terror.

Mal flew above the school and spotted Audrey perched on the parapet below, cackling at her. Now wearing a villainous black cape, Audrey looked even more diabolical than before, as if the scepter's evil venom had spread to her soul. Dragon Mal dove toward her and blasted the sorceress with her flaming breath.

Audrey blocked and deflected the flame easily with her scepter. Her sinister laugh pierced the night as she returned a flurry of savage lightning bolts to Mal.

Dragon Mal ducked and swerved, narrowly avoiding the crackling bolts. Wings pumping, she reared back and prepared to release fiery havoc on Audrey once again but jerked to a sudden stop at the sight below. Audrey had pulled Celia tight to her chest and was using the poor girl as a human shield.

"Be careful not to fry your little VK buddy," Audrey cackled vilely. Sensing victory at last, she crowed triumphantly. So this was what sweet revenge felt like. Audrey liked it.

Mal pulled back; she couldn't rout Audrey without burning Celia. *Well played, Audrey, well played,* she thought. Mal would have to find another way. If only the ember worked . . . Dragon Mal held Hades's unlit ember in her claw and breathed a fiery breath toward it, frantically trying to relight it. But the extinguished ember refused to spark.

On the ground, Uma and Harry saw the sky illuminate and watched as Dragon Mal flew in circles around the parapet, narrowly escaping the crippling jolts of Audrey's scepter. "She doesn't stand a chance without the ember," mumbled Uma. Harry had to agree—*advantage: Audrey* all the way.

On top of the parapet, Celia decided to take matters into her own hands. Using all her might, she wrenched violently and threw Audrey's aim off-kilter. "Hold still, you little brat," yelled Audrey. Celia's jerking had caused her to miss.

Audrey tightened her grip on Celia and forced Dr. Facilier's willful daughter into submission, then searched the sky, took sharp aim again, and released another round of unrelenting jolts at the soaring dragon. This time she didn't miss.

Dragon Mal's right wing took a direct hit. She reeled back, then faltered, her balance and flying skills both compromised by injury. Hope shriveled inside her. Dragon Mal dropped rapidly from the sky.

"Help me, Mal," shrieked Celia. But Mal was too riddled with injury to come to her aid. She watched helplessly as Audrey chased Celia around the parapet.

Uma pulled out her glowing shell necklace and began to shout. "Stronger together!" she screamed.

Mal looked down in total surprise and saw the pirate leader standing below with Harry Hook by her side. Mal wasn't alone. Uma, standing strong and proud, held her glowing shell necklace aloft.

"We're stronger together," Uma bellowed. "I'm right here, Mal. Regain your might and ignite." Mal had been right. Uma did care, and she wasn't going anywhere. She was standing in solidarity with her friend. "I'm right here, girl, I'm right here."

With reenergized resolve, Mal held out the unlit ember in her talon, flapped her one good wing with all her strength, and stared down intensely at Uma.

Uma looked into Mal's eyes and incanted: *"Regain your might and ignite."*

The ember in Mal's talon glowed briefly, then dimmed quickly. Mal's determination didn't waver. The doughty dragon flared her damaged wing with difficulty, and repositioned herself directly above Uma and Harry this time. Below her, Uma held out her enchanted shell necklace and locked eyes with Mal again. *"Regain your might and ignite,"* repeated Uma. Her words were charged with even more passion and conviction this time.

In a magical moment, the ember in Mal's talon flared to life. The wing she'd injured in the firefight healed. With renewed vigor, Dragon Mal spread her wings and returned to her fiery showdown against Audrey.

As Dragon Mal darted toward the parapet, she

saw Celia cowering in fear as Audrey stalked toward her. Fueled by rage, Audrey blasted Celia with a wild display of sparks that sent the young girl flying against the stone wall. "You want a piece of this?" threatened Audrey, tossing the scepter back and forth between her hands with wicked ease.

Celia crouched, cringed, and trembled. "No, no, I'm good."

Mal had seen enough. With courage and grit, Dragon Mal thrust the newly lit ember toward Audrey. Not to be outdone, Audrey thrust her scepter toward Mal. Mal's blinding blue laser and Audrey's pink lightning bolt met in the middle of the sky. The two magics locked in a power struggle.

"C'mon, Mal," cheered Celia.

"Go on, Mal," howled Harry.

"You got this, girl," Uma shouted encouragingly.

Dragon Mal's blue laser locked on to Audrey, flashed bright, then drained the sorceress of her power. Audrey felt herself weakening under the ember's crippling glow. She panicked and wailed, but it was too late. Maleficent's scepter fell from her hand to the ground with a clank. Audrey crumpled beside it, unconscious, the queen's crown no longer on her head.

Dragon Mal disappeared in a cloud of purple smoke as she landed on the stone tower. She emerged, back to human form, with her bluish-purple hair still sizzling a touch. The ember glowed in her hand.

"Mal!" Celia jumped up in joy, ran hard to Mal, and hugged her tightly.

Mal put her arm around Celia protectively. "It's okay, Celia, I got you."

Mal looked over Celia's shoulder, noticed Audrey's lifeless body, and rushed to her side, distraught. "Audrey? Audrey?" She held out the lit ember, hoping its all-powerful magic would stir Audrey awake, but nothing happened. That didn't make sense; the ember was potent enough to help. Heartsick, Mal remembered her father's grave warning: *You're only half Hades. The ember won't do everything for you that it does for me.*

Mal was crushed.

Below, Uma and Harry cheered and whooped. They'd done it . . . together. And all across Auradon,

Audrey's spelled lifted. Dizzy, Squeaky, and Squirmy came to in Evie's living room and looked around in confusion. The bewildered villain offspring didn't know what had happened, but they did know one thing: "I'm hungry," said the twins in unison. It was the first time Dizzy had heard them speak aloud to anyone other than each other.

"Same," she said. The three kids sprinted to the kitchen, poured themselves tall glasses of milk, and began devouring the final remnants of Jane's cake. They smiled happily, all three of them wearing milk mustaches.

The kids weren't the only ones unspelled. Fairy Godmother opened her eyes, surprised to find Doug, Gil, and a very relieved Jane sitting in front of her on the museum steps. "Oooh. Bibbidi-bobbidi what happened?" she asked, slightly befuddled.

Jane jumped up and embraced her mom. "The spell's been broken. It's okay," Jane told her. She had so much to tell her mom.

Outside Fairy Cottage, Evie, Jay, Carlos, Ben, and Dude were transformed back from stone. "Mal must have defeated Audrey," said Evie. She was relieved about that but still felt tinges of hurt.

"C'mon, let's go," said a clean-shaven and fangless Ben. They raced off toward Auradon Prep, eager to find Mal and hear the details of how she'd brought down Audrey.

A short time later, everyone gathered in Audrey's dorm room. Anguish and despair hovered in the air. Mal and Evie kept constant vigil by Audrey's bedside, where she lay motionless. "She's slipping away," Evie said.

Mal bit her lip in thought. "There's only one person in the world who might be able to do something about this. And that's Hades."

"Hades!" exclaimed Ben, thinking back to the horrifying battle on the bridge. That was not a scene the king wished to repeat. "He wouldn't do it, and I wouldn't risk it."

"Actually, he might do it for me," said Mal. She took a deep breath. It was time to share her deepest secret with her fiancé and friends. "He's my father."

Jay and Carlos exchanged shocked looks. Neither of them had had any idea. Although that did explain Mal's temper.

Ben was hit with a sudden bolt of understanding, but even with this new information, he wasn't completely comfortable with the idea. Ben looked into Mal's eyes. Her face was set with certainty; saving Audrey was worth the risk. "I'll have to send guards to get him," Ben said.

Uma stepped forward, the seashells on her shirt clattering. "Maybe I can hitch a ride."

Mal looked at her questioningly.

"The Isle is my home. And someone needs to take care of it," Uma said bravely.

"Well then, you'll need a first mate." Harry placed both of his hands on her shoulders, ever loyal.

Mal nodded, moved by their selfless sacrifice. True leaders made tough choices. "Well then, the Isle will be in very good hands," Mal said, realizing she was sad to lose her new friends.

Celia asked Mal, "Can I go, too?" Celia said she liked Auradon—it was just that she missed her dad too much. "Wish I could be in both places," she added wistfully.

Mal wished that, too. She turned to Uma and Harry, her voice filled with sincerity. "I really think Evie was right. I do think that we could have been friends. I'm really sorry I lied to all of you guys. You deserve so much better than that."

Jay jumped in. "You were just trying to do the right thing."

Mal looked at Jay, ever grateful for his friendship. One by one, each of the kids, even Uma and Harry, nodded at Mal with forgiveness.

"Yeah," agreed Uma with a small smile.

Evie was the last holdout. Mal turned to her BFF, her eyes brimming with hope. Finally, Evie nodded. "I get it," she said.

They really were all stronger together.

CHAPTER TWENTY-ONE

A VILLAIN HAS ARRIVED IN AURADON TO SAVE THE DAY! WHO WOULD HAVE THOUGHT? CRAZY, RIGHT?

A looming black SUV pulled into the Auradon Prep circular drive. Four commanding officers of the Auradon Royal Guard stepped out. One opened the rear door while flanked by the other three, who stood ready to surround the obviously dangerous passenger. Hades's feet, which were locked together in chains, hit the pavement with a clank.

Upstairs, Audrey lay stiff and lifeless in her dorm room bed, looking every bit a princess once more with her pink gown and long brushed hair. Queen Leah, grief-stricken, sat beside her motionless grand-daughter and held her hand. Fairy Godmother and

Belle stood attentively on Audrey's other side. Beast paced the rug a few feet away.

There was a knock at the door. Mal, wearing a subdued lavender shirt and a tasteful gold skirt, jumped to open it. But Beast beat her to it.

Hades stood towering in the doorway, legs shackled, hands cuffed, and guards on all sides. The officers escorted him into the room. The god of the Underworld's menacing presence sent an uncomfortable ripple through the air. Everyone was clearly on edge.

"Thank you for coming," said Mal with an efficient nod. A dragon barrette pulled her bluish-purple hair back neatly into a low ponytail. As she stood close to Hades, the family resemblance was unmistakable.

"Didn't have much choice," said Hades, his shackles clanging. He looked about the opulent dorm room, with its gold brocade chairs and rose wallpaper. He had to hand it to the good guys: they were sure living the sweet life in Auradon.

"Can you wake her?" asked Ben.

"Since when do heroes care about villains?" hissed Hades, danger clear in his voice.

"She's . . ." Ben stopped and realized there was no good answer for that.

"One of your own. Right. When you guys try to destroy the world, it's an error in judgment. But when it's one of us, lock 'em up and throw away the key." Hades leveled a look at Beast. There was no love lost for the man who had permanently banished him and every other villain to the Isle. "Right, Beast?" he said with a snicker.

Mal registered the troubling double standard and furrowed her brow. Hades had a point. It did seem terribly unfair.

Suddenly, Hades jerked his arms in the air. Everyone startled in fear.

"I'm going to need my hands," Hades said.

With apprehension, Mal signaled for his release. She'd learned from Uma to trust that sometimes help came from the most unexpected places.

The tension in the room rose as Hades rubbed his wrists together, then held out his hand, ready to reclaim his unrivaled object of power. Mal gave Hades the glowing ember. His hair burst into blue flames, and the ember burned even brighter.

"I haven't lost my touch," remarked Hades, relishing the feeling of the magic as it ran through his veins. For the first time in a long while, he felt whole. Hades moseyed right up to Beast, stared into his eyes, and growled. With his peerless powers restored, Hades could defeat Beast in one quick blast. Beast didn't flinch. He, too, unleashed an intimidating guttural roar. The two men stood nose to nose, both ready to pounce at a moment's notice.

"Dad," Mal said quietly.

Hades studied the pleading expression on his daughter's face, then reluctantly acceded. He pulled himself away from Beast and moved to Audrey's bedside. Queen Leah, clearly terror-stricken in Hades's presence, stayed by Audrey's side and clutched her granddaughter's hand protectively.

Hades held the glowing ember above Audrey and swirled it through the air. Under Hades's command, the ember emitted a dark whirlpool of colors, which grew progressively lighter and brighter. As Hades worked his magic, pulsating shafts of colored light moved through the room. With a flash of brilliant blue light, Audrey awakened with a stretch, as if she'd just woken from the most peaceful nap.

Hades tossed the ember into the air like *It ain't no big thing. I just saved the girl, or whatever.*

Queen Leah sobbed with relief and clasped her granddaughter. "Audrey, you're okay," she cried.

Audrey noticed Mal and Ben, and her face flooded with shame. "Tell me it was all a bad dream," she said.

"I wish I could," said Ben. "But it's over now." He tried to sound reassuring.

"I'm sorry. I wanted to hurt you both. I wanted to hurt all of you," Audrey admitted, mortified by her actions.

Audrey moved to the edge of the bed toward Mal, who took her hand and looked at her solemnly. Audrey wasn't the only one who was sorry. "I have owed you an apology for a very long time now," said Mal with heartfelt realization. She'd love-spelled Ben and never looked back.

"So have I," added Ben.

Audrey's face filled with light.

Queen Leah stepped to Mal. "And perhaps I've owed you one as well." Queen Leah gave the slightest curtsy and bowed her head a touch. One small bow from Queen Leah was a giant step for villainkind. Mal returned the curtsy.

As everyone fawned over Audrey, the guards re-handcuffed Hades, then led the dangerous captive back into the Auradon Prep hallway. Mal struggled to find her words. "Dad," she yelped. Hades took a step toward his daughter, but the guards restrained him from getting any closer.

"I'm going to miss you all over again," she said. He'd come through for her when she needed him.

Hades shrugged sheepishly. "Thanks for a glimpse of the sun," he said. The lines around his eyes crinkled as he smiled.

Mal watched as he was led down the hall, once again a captive on his way to permanent imprisonment on the Isle. She smoothed her hand over her purple-and-blue hair, went to his side, and surprised him with a kiss on the cheek. Hades turned his back to her and opened his left hand, which held the ember. Mal took it and held it close. As he continued down the hall, Hades turned back for one last look at his daughter and left her with a knowing wink.

CHAPTER TWENTY-TWO

THE THING IS I DON'T THINK I CAN BE THE QUEEN OF AURADON EVERYONE EXPECTS ME TO BE. I CAN ONLY BE THE KIND OF QUEEN THAT'S TRUE TO ME.

One week later, Mal and Ben's engagement party was in full swing on the multileveled terrace overlooking Auradon's Bridge Plaza. In contrast to the Isle's dilapidated Bridge Plaza, Auradon's was a magnificent tree-lined court with four decks connected by blue carpet-lined stairs. It was the ideal setting to celebrate the joyful occasion.

Mal was the picture of grace in a metallic-orchid dress, elbow-length lilac gloves, gold peep-toe booties, and a gold tiara with purple and blue stones. Ben also looked dashing in a sharp three-piece blue suit sans tie. He took Mal's arm in his, and together the gorgeous couple walked through the tunnel and into the party in progress.

"There they are," announced Evie, who gave off an air of sophistication in a structured midnight-blue gown of her own design. She looked at Doug, who stood by her side in a mint-green suit and blue shirt. Mal and Ben weren't the only ones in love.

Mal and Ben grinned at their friends, then at each other as they took in the festive scene. Uniformed waiters circulated throughout the plaza, balancing silver trays piled with gourmet canapés. Jubilant party guests in chic cocktail dresses and stylish sport coats mixed and mingled. Dizzy, dressed to the nines in a black-and-moss polka-dot frock, spun between Squeaky and Squirmy, who both wore blue-and-white-striped tailcoats. The swanky event was a definite first for the impoverished Isle kids.

Mal waved to the guests, then smiled kindly at Audrey. It was Audrey's first public appearance since her recent touch with evil, and she looked herself again in a beaded pink off-the-shoulder dress and her demure bluebird necklace.

Ben kissed Mal's hand, then escorted her up

the stairs to the plaza's balcony. The king clinked his crystal punch glass to get everyone's attention. "Lady Mal and I want to thank you for celebrating our engagement with us today," he told the crowd, before turning toward his future bride. "I couldn't be prouder or happier to call you my queen." With a wide smile, he looked back at the celebrating masses. "So raise your glasses to our future queen of Auradon!"

The guests all raised their glasses high in the air. "To our queen of Auradon."

"Speech, Your Specialness," shouted Carlos, all dressed up in a black-and-white paisley jacket and skinny-cut black pants. Smitten, Jane stood by his side in a cornflower lace midi-dress and her one-of-a-kind Jarlos necklace.

"Speech, oh fancy one," yelled Jay, laughing. The gold embroidery on his sport coat reflected the glow of the twinkle lights. With his hair tied up in a tidy man bun, he clapped for Mal. She deserved all of it.

Mal looked at the expectant faces that surrounded her, especially those of the villain kids. She shook her head. "I can't. I can't be queen of Auradon."

The room stirred. Evie gasped. Ben's face dropped.

"I can't turn my back on the Isle," Mal explained to him quietly.

She addressed the crowd again. "We made a decision to close the barrier forever. It was my idea. But it's wrong," she admitted. "I've learned that you can't live in fear. Because it doesn't actually protect you from anything. You never know where the bad is going to come from. And you never know where the heroes are going to come from, either. Without Uma and her pirates, Auradon would be gone. And without Hades, my father, Audrey would be gone."

The crowd reeled at this new revelation. Mal absorbed their reactions and continued. "We are all capable of good and bad, no matter which side of the barrier we come from." She raised her head with the clear insight and strength of a leader who was able to see the complete nature of her people for the first time.

Jay, Evie, and Carlos beamed with pride at their friend.

Mal turned to King Ben with conviction. She took both his hands in hers. "And that's why I can't be queen of just Auradon. I have to be queen of the Isle, too. It's time we take the barrier down. Forever."

"We can't do that," said Beast, alarmed at the mere suggestion.

Ben stood shoulder to shoulder with his queen and looked at his father. "It's up to us, Dad. I choose to be a king who moves forward. It's time for forgiveness. It's time for new beginnings. The barrier will come down." It was an official royal proclamation. Auradon and the Isle would be united as one.

"Yes! Woo-hooo-hoooo!" whooped Carlos with unabashed glee.

Doug, Jane, and the crowd hooted and cheered. Evie, Jay, and Carlos were ecstatic and moved by the historic event. Even Chad, Audrey, and Queen Leah, who had a new empathy for villains, applauded.

Ben smiled proudly and gave the honor of dismantling the barrier to the future queen of the United States of Auradon. "Bring it down, Mal."

Fairy Godmother offered Mal her wand with a warm smile. Mal took the enchanted wand and studied it in her hands. She couldn't believe there had been a time, not so long before, when her only goal on Auradon had been to steal that very wand. Opening the barrier might bring others who looked to do the same, but Mal, with the help of her friends, would find a way to deal with the occasional evil as it arose.

Mal held the wand in her hand, then looked to Jay, Evie, and Carlos. This honor wasn't hers alone; they had achieved the opening of the Isle together. The four of them had made this dream a reality. Mal asked Jay, Evie, and Carlos to join her up on the balcony. The four original VKs stood together. It was their proudest moment. *"To make the world a better place . . ."* Mal incanted.

"We have to do it face to face," Mal, Evie, Jay, and Carlos spoke in unison.

Mal's eyes briefly flashed green. She twirled her hands in the air, then waved the wand at the Isle of the Lost. With a crackle, the barrier, which for so long had separated the Isle from Auradon, began to come down. It popped, shattered, then exploded into a brilliant shower of emeralds that rained into the sea. The divider between the two lands was no more.

With a grateful smile, Mal used the wand again. She moved her hands to create a dazzling bridge that stretched from the Auradon City shore to the Isle of the Lost. It was a bridge anyone could cross at any time. The island was no longer a prison. All the VKs of the Isle were free.

On the dilapidated Isle streets, elated villain kids celebrated. They'd been liberated! Without the barrier to act as shade, rays of sunshine broke through the gloom and shone down on the Isle.

Uma threw her arms out wide and spun around triumphantly. "My plan," she said, and it was. Ben had been right: Uma was part of the solution. "Yeeesss!" she exclaimed as she bounded up the stairs. Uma stood on the balcony above the Isle's Bridge Plaza and looked across the sea at Mal, who stood on a parallel balcony in Auradon. From Uma's perspective, Mal had done right by the Isle kids in the end. The dragon girl had redeemed herself.

Mal looked back across the sea and smiled at Uma with utmost appreciation. When Mal had been in her most desperate moment, Uma had stepped up and helped. For that, Mal would be eternally grateful. The two really weren't all that different from each other. Both young women were bold leaders who were trying to do good while still being true to themselves. From across the water, they shared a knowing nod; they were stronger together.

Evie, Jay, Carlos, and Ben surrounded Mal on the Auradon terrace balcony while Harry, Gil, and Celia rallied around Uma on the Isle. Both groups frolicked, danced, and paraded toward the center of the bridge. There the two crews abandoned their irreconcilable differences and formed one indivisible team.

Everything went quiet once the Isle kids reached Auradon. King Ben stood before the people of Auradon, looked at Mal and the throngs of villain offspring behind her, and took a knee before the Isle kids. The Auradon citizens followed his lead and bowed to the VKs.

After a moment of utter disbelief, the VKs swarmed the plaza in jubilation, whooping, hollering, and living it up. With Auradon and the Isle united at last, everyone—whoever they were, wherever they were from—threw their arms in the air and danced and sang with unbridled happiness.

Evie and Jay clutched each other with a joy more

intense than they'd ever felt before. Chad and Audrey hugged, both ready for a new day. Mal threw her arms around Dizzy and Celia, then watched as they grabbed Squeaky and Squirmy and ran to hug Dr. Facilier, Lady Tremaine, and Smee.

Carlos and Jane held hands, the perfect picture of Isle and Auradon come together. An idea crossed Jane's mind, and a look of trepidation fell over her face. "Carlos, I'm actually really nervous to meet your mom."

"*You're* nervous? It's Cruella De Vil. I'm petrified," Dude chimed in. Cruella's reputation for a hatred of animals preceded her.

"Wait till she hears I want to be a vet," said Carlos. He knew his mom would freak out. And for the first time in his life, he was okay with that.

Jay turned to Gil with wide open eyes. "What do you say you and me go exploring?" he asked. "I'll take a gap year."

Jay had been in Auradon all this time and had barely ventured off campus. And when he did, it was only for away games. Wasn't seeing the world the reason he'd wanted off the Isle in the first place? All that was left to decide was where to go first. "Jungles or icebergs?"

"Both!" exclaimed Gil. He threw his hands up, overjoyed. He couldn't wait to see all the wonders of Auradon with his new friend. "Chest bump," he yelled. He and Jay met midair, thrilled about the escapades that lay ahead.

Evie, Uma, Harry, and Doug stood nearby. Uma looked at Mal, who was busy greeting new Isle kids. "Mal came through," she said.

"She always does," said Evie. No matter what, Mal always did the right thing in the end.

Harry stared at Mal with his striking green eyes. "She's definitely taken, right?"

"Definitely," Evie said with a nod.

Doug stepped up next to Evie and put his arm around his true love. "So's Evie."

Uma, in a high-necked aqua dress and leather bodice, put her hands on her hips and cocked her head. "What's my name?"

Harry did a double take, raised his eyebrows, and beamed at Uma. "Uma." He leaned in flirtatiously for a kiss.

"Uh-uh," said Uma, dissing him.

No matter: Harry spun around to find Audrey standing before him. The pirate's interest in the pink princess was immediately piqued.

Mal and Ben searched the crowd and spotted Hades, who was hard to miss with his blue hair. The father and daughter walked toward each other. "Am I invited to your wedding?" asked the father of the bride.

"Hi, Dad," Ben said, trying out the new moniker on his future father-in-law. It sounded awkward.

Mal ran to Hades, bridging the difference, and, for the first time ever, publicly hugged her father. At first Hades stood with his arms stiff at his sides. He'd never been on the receiving end of such an embrace; he didn't know what to do. Then, instinctually, the villain raised his hands and hugged Mal back.

"I'm sure you'll be very happy together," said Hades.

Ben turned to Mal and wrapped her up in his arms in a loving embrace. Over Mal's shoulder, Hades gave Ben the *I'm watching you* gesture. Ben smiled, not sure if the god of the Underworld was kidding.

"Welcome to Auradon," Ben said as he patted Hades on the back. Hades glared at him. This relationship was going to take a little bit of getting used to. Okay, a lot of getting used to.

Mal locked eyes with Evie, who then locked eyes with Jay, who looked to Carlos. Without saying a word, the four friends took a moment to celebrate what they had accomplished. The VKs strode to each other and linked arms. They looked out over the new bridge toward the Isle of the Lost.

"You ever miss them?" asked Evie, talking about their villain parents, who were still on the Isle.

"Yeah," admitted Jay.

"Do you think they miss us?" Mal wondered aloud.

"Yeah, of course," answered Carlos.

"'Cuz we're rotten," said Mal.

"To the core," said the four as one, laughing.

"Hey," said Carlos, "the last one over the bridge . . ."

"Is a rotten apple," shouted the foursome as they ran full speed ahead for home.